ST. THOMAS CHURCH

HOW WE ALL HAVE FALLEN SHORT

ST. THOMAS CHURCH

HOW WE ALL HAVE FALLEN SHORT

Da Me

ARPress
45 Dan Road Suite 5
Canton MA 02021
Hotline: 1(888) 821-0229
Fax: 1(508) 545-7580

Ordering Information:
Quantity sales. Special discounts are available on quantity purchases by corporations, associations, and others. For details, contact the publisher at the address above.

Printed in the United States of America.

ISBN-13: Softcover   979-8-89356-610-9
          Hardcover   979-8-89356-611-6
          eBook   979-8-89356-612-3

Library of Congress Control Number: 2024903502

A special thanks is given to Dave Sumner for helping with the research.

Dedicated to all pastors everywhere who expect nothing less than the very best from their people for, the best deserves nothing less.

TABLE OF CONTENTS

PROLOGUE

In an of out of the way part of northwestern Michigan lies the small town of Hartlin, Michigan. Hartlin was so small there was only one church for the whole community. This is the story of that church and the people who call it home. The name of that church is St. Thomas Church. This church could be any church on this little planet we call home, for the purpose of consideration please think of it as your own. If you do not have a church to call home, please, feel free to watch the events unfold.

This novel is not a true story however, it is a book about truth. St. Thomas Church has a lot of dirty laundry to hang out to dry as we do and shall hang theirs for all to see. Many outside the church say, "Christians are just a bunch of hypocrites who want to be viewed as holier than thou." For some of us that just might be correct. But if we are honest with ourselves we must admit that the only difference between a believer and a non-believer that is we know that we need help and that the only person that can help us is our LORD and Savior Jesus Christ

In order to tell these people 's stories correctly this book may seem like a soap opera. Yet, please don't let that scare you off for even though this is a book about one church's love for those within and outside their borders. It is meant as a book that that should make you think and question what you are doing and what you believe. Lastly, I wrote this book to show what true forgiveness looks like.

All references in this book will be in either New International Version (NIV) or New Living Translation (NLT) and will be noted as *NIV **NLT

Chapter 1

Modern Day

Hartlin is a nice peaceful village in North Western Michigan. It was a town; right out of some old fifty's family television show. This town was so small it only had one church that lay in the center of the village. From the outside it looked perfect, too perfect nevertheless its members knew the truth. St. Thomas was far from perfect, as it is the case in all churches.

Pastor Steve Palmer was the pastor of St. Thomas Church. He was a tall slender young unmarried man, whose looks could make any girl's heart skip a beat yet, he was a very humble Godly man. His head knowledge and passion for the LORD's word was to be envied. On the other hand, when it came to street smarts he was lacking.

Every Sunday Pastor Steve Palmer ended the service like a coach giving a pep talk to his players, "Now go out there and show your friends and family who Christ really is!" He frequently wondered (and for good reason, for his fears were accurate), "does my congregation actually hear what I am saying or are my words just going in one ear and out the other." He felt that if his parishioners were just sitting in the pews out of duty and to make themselves feel good, he was wasting his time. Nevertheless, he felt that he had to try and wake these people up from their inaction.

The people left as always, very cordially everyone shook the pastor's hand as if it were a ticket to leave. Brenda Horn could not help but stare in disdainful disbelief at Jason Rainer. A girl had her hand in

Jason's back jean pocket, then he slipped his in hers with this the girl let out a girlish giggle. "What do those girls see in Jason Rainer?", said Brenda Horn, who was the youth pastor of the church. She was a tall, nerdy looking woman who was far more conservative than you would ever expect from a youth pastor in her early 20s. But, she loved her teens. Her friend replied, "Don't those girls see he is just using them? They hang all over him like he is some pop star," Brenda said. "In my day a girl who gave away her virginity as willingly as these girls are giving it to Jason would destroy their reputation! Today these girls brag about losing their virginity, and many say it was to Jason. If I ever met the devil in the flesh, I say it would have to be him." Jason wasn't always a bad boy and in reality, he wasn't truly the devil incarnate as his youth pastor proposed he was just a hurt young man.

Twenty Years Earlier

Samantha, like most little girls dreamed of marrying her Prince charming. In college, she thought she had found her prince in Isaac Rainer. He was a tall muscular basketball player. He was the kind of guy that could make any girl's knees go weak. With his athletic ability, his education was all paid for so he never gave it much thought. Then in one sad life-changing moment everything went bad.

He was out drinking with some buddies when one of them suggested let us see who has the fastest car. Isaac loved his car. It was his most prized possession, and he loves showing off what she could do, so he told his friends, "You're on, prepare to eat my dust!" The drunken racers met at the last traffic light before leaving town. They revved their engines, and as soon as the light turned green, they gunned it. But in less than 30 seconds Isaac's life changed forever.

Isaac and his friends were speeding down Main Street when a passing car appeared out of nowhere. Isaac's friends were unable to stop in time to avoid hitting the passing car. Yet, Isaac who was drunk (had delayed reaction time) plowed into his friend's car. The damage to his body was worse than the damage to his car. Isaac's legs were crushed so he could never play basketball again. Since they were both drunk, neither dared call the cops. (But of course, the police came anyways) so, both of them were charged with matching pairs of DUI, so their insurance companies wouldn't pay for the damage.

If that wasn't bad enough, since he couldn't play basketball anymore. He couldn't pay for college. He was forced to swallow his pride and admit the jam he got himself into. However, his father reluctantly gave Isaac a job at his auto repair shop. All this heartache could have pushed Samantha away from the bad boy Isaac had become. However, it made him even more attractive to her and Isaac wasn't about to let a good-looking girl like Samantha, get away. As long as the relationship was fun, he was willing to hang on.

After a few months, it became clear that Samantha was hoping to get her MRS degree, so he proposed and shortly after she graduated from college they were married. It wasn't long after this that Samantha became pregnant with their first child, a boy was born. They named the boy Jason. Samantha loved the idea of being a wife and a mother yet, something seemed off. She and Isaac didn't seem to be connecting as they used to. Nothing has changed but he was still the same selfish, bitter man that he always was. He couldn't forgive himself for that drunken drag race that ruined his life.

Everything came to a head one stressful morning. Soon after Amber, their second child, was born. Jason was about four years old at the time so he was loud and rambunctious. Amber was less than a year old, so to her parents it felt like all she ever did was cry. Samantha needed help with the children yet, her husband wasn't giving her any help. She kept telling him things she needed him to do. Isaac didn't even know where to start so when Samantha said "just go get me some milk!" Isaac left and never returned. She worried about him but, after several months of the police looking for him, it became clear that Isaac just abandoned his family and did not want to be found Samantha, filed for divorce.

A few months after Samantha filed for divorce two police officers came to her door. They rang the doorbell. When she came to the door they asked her, "Are you Mrs. Samantha Rainer?" She responded, "Yes, although I recently divorced my husband." The officers said, "Your ex-husband's body has been found. It appears he rolled his car some time ago." At hearing this Samantha broke down crying.

It was difficult at first but now that she knew her husband would never be returning she felt more at peace. After moving into a more affordable upstairs apartment in Hartlin, getting a new job in New New Deli, Michigan they did okay at least financially. But, Samantha had no clue how bad this was hurting Jason emotionally.

Three Years Ago

Jason was a 16-year-old sophomore in high school. One day a beautiful tall girl with the loveliest long blonde locks, named Elizabeth, asked him, "Jason, would you like to come over to my house to study?" Jason wasn't quite sure how to respond. He said, "ah? Sure." Both teenagers were kind of hoping for something more than a study date yet, they were not comfortable sharing what was on their minds.

That first study date went well, so did the next few study dates. Then one afternoon it all changed when Elizabeth's parents had to go out suddenly, but they trust Jason and their daughter. They shouldn't have, because one thing led to another before either of them came to their senses, they had given up a precious gift with each other. The next day, word had spread about what they had done. Neither of them wanted to talk about what happened. Jason became very popular with the girls in the school for, like his father, he became a bad boy. At first, he just wanted to be with Elizabeth but she was too embarrassed to see Jason. On the other hand, many other girls gave him attention that was too great to ignore.

Girls were freely giving themselves to him, just to say they have been with this bad boy. His social life was so great but his home life couldn't have been worse. His sister thought he was a pig for taking advantage of those girls who clearly don't have much self-respect. His mom tried to talk to him about how he was treating these girls yet, as you can imagine he didn't want to talk about sex with his mom.

Samantha felt like she was at her wits end. So, she shared with a friend about her concerns and her friend said, "what about your ex-husband, can't he talk to his son about this." Samantha replied, "He's dead. He died when the kids were just babies." Her friend said, "What about a boyfriend or some other male role model for your son." Samantha said, "If Jason had a male role model don't you think I would have that person talk to Jason!" Then Samantha's friend said, "Well your family should check my church out. There are many godly men at my church who could take Jason under their wing." Samantha realized her friend was trying a little too hard to get her to come to her church. Nevertheless, she had grown up in a church that so believed that divorce was wrong that, that church body rejected anyone that was divorced. Therefore, she feared that her family would not be welcome. But, her friend was aware of Samantha's family's situation as a result Samantha gave her friend's church a chance. Samantha asked, "What church do you go to?", she asked. Her friend replied, "St. Thomas Church.

So that Sunday, Samantha and her family check the church out. Jason said he felt very uncomfortable there yet, Amber and Samantha felt it was a breath of fresh air. Samantha was delighted to see how accepting this church made her feel (even after they learned that she was a divorcee.) Many of the elderly men of this church offered to mentor Jason; however, that only made Jason long even more for his father. These men were nice yet they were so old they felt more like grandfather figures than any father. One day Jason asked one of these men why they were giving him so much attention. They responded, "Well, I would like to see you become the man, I know you can be." Jason snapped, "You mean you are sorry for me because I don't have a dad!" The man tried to reassure Jason that this was not the case, by saying, "No Jason! I believe and so does everyone else here, who has been trying to take you under their wing, you can become a great man. The Apostle Paul talks in Titus

2 about how older men should mentor younger men and younger women should be mentored by older women. So, half heartily Jason agreed to be mentored. Still, in his mind he was thinking, "This is going to be a waste of time."

In a year's time Jason only became worse. As for Samantha, she was dating a nice handsome godly widower named Michael. So, she asked her boyfriend to go talk to Jason. So, Michael and his son Gregory (amber's boyfriend) took Jason out for breakfast. The purpose for this little intervention which was no surprise to Jason. As Michael started to speak, Jason said, "I don't want to hear it. Mom and Amber say I act like a pig! Nevertheless, I don't do anything to a girl that she doesn't ask me to do! Besides, Michael you have no right to criticize me. First off, you ain't my dad, and whenever you and mom are together you can't keep your hands off of each other." Michael responded, "You are right, I probably should not be so physical with your mom. However, I know where the line is and I bet you also know where it is. Just because a girl lets you have sex with her doesn't mean you should accept the offer. I would love to make love with your mom. But, as the man in this relationship it is my honor and privilege to protect your mom, you kids and myself. So even if she wanted to go to bed with me, I would refuse."

Jason thought, "Yeah right. What guy would pass up sex? Well maybe Gregory would, but there is something not quite right about that boy. Amber and Gregory say they are involved but they don't even kiss or hold hands. I would call that just friends."

Discussion questions

1. How should you act towards people who act immoral? Are you showing a Christ like attitude towards these people?

2. How do you forgive yourself for past mistakes? What is the cost for holding on to the pain?

3. Why is it so important for a child to have a father figure in their life?

 4. Is it a man's responsibility to protect the woman he is involved with even if they are not married? (Ruth 3:7-18)

5. How are we supposed to handle problem children? How do we support other Christians who are dealing with problem children? (Luke 15:11-32, Hebrews 12:4-11)

6. How does your Church treat divorced people?

Chapter 2

Amber was as much of a romantic as her mother, but for her marriage was just an idealistic dream. Nothing that she ever saw lived out. Her mother worked all the time so she never had time to date. All Amber and Jason's friends were children from broken homes.

As a result, when aunt Mandy (not their real aunt but, a close friend of their mother) invited them to church. Amber was amazed to see men showing love and respect to their wives and children. She wondered if these men were putting on an act for their church friends but, she sure hoped they weren't. She wanted to marry a man like one of those guys someday. Although, she feared that if her mom couldn't find a guy who had the guts to not run away from his family, what chance did she have?

On Amber's first day of high school a very cute but shy boy named Gregory passed her a note, it said, "Hello Amber, my name is Gregory, I Think I've seen you at church. I was wondering if you will allow me to walk you home. On the way home I'll buy you some ice cream.

Sincerely, Gregory Mitchell"

Amber felt very flattered not only because he was extremely handsome but, because she liked what she knew about him personally. He was a very nice guy. So, despite how unsure she was she shook her head yes.

Gregory met Amber outside of her last class. When they got outside, Amber called her mom to let her know she would be late getting home. Her mother said, "Okay honey just be home by five,

I should have dinner on the table by then." Amber replied, "okay I should have no problem getting home by then. See you later mom. I love you." However, Amber had so much fun talking to Gregory that, she lost track of time. By the time she checked a clock, it was 6 PM. She screamed, "oh no, mom is going to ground me for sure! I had a great time. I hope you had a good time since we will not be seeing each other outside of school and church for quite some time!" Then she ran home as fast as she could. As she expected, her mom was mad. "Young lady, you said you were going to be home by five and it is after 6 o'clock at night! You had me worried. What do you have to say for yourself?!" exclaimed her mother. Amber knew she had no good excuse so she just apologized and explain what happened. "I have no excuse. I had such a good time talking to Gregory I lost track of time. Mother you have every right to ground me, yet I cry out for mercy." Then her mother said, "Kid I know what it is like to be a fifteen-year-old girl. Your punishment is next time you guys see each other you bring him over here so I can meet him. I would have liked to have met him in the first place. Just do a better job of keeping track of time."

Amber called Gregory up and said, "hey Gregory guess what? I'm not grounded but mom wants to meet you. Are you free next Saturday?" Gregory said, "Yeah" "great then we can watch a movie and then have lunch", replied Amber. Gregory felt uncomfortable with how pushy Amber was being but, then again, he wasn't used to any girl giving him so much attention. He was very shy and it seemed to him that the girls were always attracted to the jocks and bad boys. Neither of which he was. Yet, the fact that Gregory was a nice guy is what Amber found so appealing.

When Gregory showed up, he handed a bouquet of flowers to Samantha "Miss Rainer these are for you." Samantha thanked him for the flowers but, he seemed like a bit of a brownnoser by doing this. So, she became rather suspicious of him after watching the movie, Samantha invited Gregory, Amber and Jason to the table for lunch. However just as she called her son to the table, he headed out saying, "no thanks, I'll be eating at Kim's." Samantha would have stopped her son but, she felt like she had lost control of him. She told her daughter and her daughter's date that she thought it would be fun to make a homemade pizza. Amber felt like her mom was hijacking her date however, at the same time she had to admit it was a good idea. The kids had fun and never felt closer. When the pizza was done, they sat down and ate it and this is when Samantha's questioning started. She asked him where he knew Amber from. He said, "School and I've seen your family at church, but somehow we keep missing each other." Then Samantha asked about what his parents did for a living. Gregory said, "My dad is an architect." Amber knowing the next question her mom was going to ask, gave her a look to say, "don't ask it, you really don't want to ask it." Yet, Samantha asked it any ways, "What does your mom do for a living?" Gregory looked down in sadness and said, "Well, she is dead, she died of liver cancer. I suppose she is in heaven worshiping Jesus." In a weird way this kind of made Samantha jealous, for if her husband had died (before walking out on the family) at least she wouldn't feel like such a failure as a wife.

Samantha asked other questions about Gregory's interests and home life. She discovered that he claimed to be just a shy nerdy homebody. Not the kind of guy she would have been into when she was in high school. This guy seemed too good to be true. So, she said, "Gregory how about you and your father come over for dinner next week sometime?" Samantha was surprised when her daughter was thrilled to have Gregory's father over for a meal so she said, "I can get his number for you." Amber was excited because she liked Gregory so much. Although, Gregory wasn't so comfortable because he felt like things were moving too fast. As a result, he spoke up and said, "Whoa whoa whoa Miss Rainer I'm feeling a little uncomfortable! May I please speak to your daughter in private for a moment?" Therefore, Samantha said they could talk in the hallway that divides the different apartments so that is just what they did. Gregory said,

"Amber this is only our second date and I feel like you and your mom are interviewing me to be your husband. I know I'm the guy so I expect to be interrogated but, wanting to meet my dad! Fine, if your mom wants to meet him, no skin off my back. However, that seems like a step that would suggest this relationship was more serious than I was counting on." Amber felt like he was making more out of this than he had to, but she wasn't going to say anything about that because she had her own issues. Amber said, "Okay I can respect that, I have my own issues I need to talk to you about. You know how you tried to put your arm around me during the movie but, I moved away?" Gregory said, "Yes, I noticed and that is what confuses me. You and your mother talk as if we are far more serious than I thought we were but, you don't want me to hold you?" Amber said, "I do care about you and I want our relationship to grow yet, with my issues of growing up without a dad and seeing my brother's promiscuity. I would rather avoid the physical side of the dating relationship." Gregory said, "that's cool I can respect that."

That following week when she met Michael (Gregory's Father), she was impressed to say the least. He was a handsome, kind, soft-spoken man. When he arrived, he said, "Hello you must be Mrs. Rainer." Samantha said, "and you must be Gregory's father, please come in." After Mr. Mitchell came in she said, "Your son seems like a nice young man, to be honest you seem too nice to believe. I had to meet the man who raise this gentleman." With a slight chuckle, Michael said, "Yeah that's my Gregory."

Samantha invited her guest to sit down and enjoy the meal she prepared. Not quite sure what to say to break the ice. She said to Michael, "so Gregory says you are a widower. Have you dated much since your wife died?" Michael said, "No between work and home there hasn't been much time for a social life. What about you? Have you dated much?" Samantha responded, "Mean neither on top of not having time, being abandoned by my husband sure sours a woman's taste for men. No offense. Then he reassured her, "if I was in your place, I would feel the same way. So, I take no offense. I apologize on the behalf of all men. Some guys can be such jerks. Some of us just don't know how to treasure a beautiful person like you Samantha, if I may be so forward as to call you by your first name." Jason who was there couldn't believe any man would speak such dribble unless he was trying to get into a woman's pants. As he sat there, he was thinking, "This guy better not be thinking about getting with my mom. Hey, she is my mom how gross can you get! Besides it is rude to hoard in on his sister's date. Amber and Gregory were glad to see their parents getting along so well. However, with their laughter and carrying on, it was hard for the teens to get a word in edgewise. When they did, it was mostly small talk. As the night was ending Michael said, "I've had a nice time tonight. I'm hoping I am not being to presumptuous Samantha; would you like to go out sometime?" When Samantha heard these words, she, felt like a teenage girl being asked to the prom by the cutest boy in school. She wanted to scream, "Yes, yes, yes a thousand times yes!" But she was a grown woman with grown-up responsibilities and besides, she wasn't sure it would be appropriate being that Michael was the father of her daughter's boyfriend. She said "I'd love to but I'm very busy as a nurse and mother. About the only free time I have is the half hour I get for lunch." Michael being determined to see this lovely woman again said, "That works. When do you have lunch?" Samantha said, "Around 11:45." Then Michael said, "Okay, I'll bring a lunch we can share." Samantha said, "That will work yet, won't it be weird for the kids." Amber was thinking, "of course it will be weird to have my boyfriend's father dating my mom nevertheless, my mom deserves to be happy too." So, she said, "mom if you like this guy give him a chance." Gregory told his father, "Amber's mom is a babe if you like her go for it."

Michael met Samantha at the hospital. He brought a large sub sandwich for them to share and some pop. Samantha loved sitting outside talking and getting to know Michael better. However, she kept fearing that he would lose track of time and that she would be late getting back to work. She was never late but they never had enough time together either. After a week, she said, "This is crazy you and Gregory should come over for dinner." From then on, every spare moment they had they were together.

Since they went to the same church people started gossiping about them. Many people at their church said, "they are always together acting like a family and being very affectionate." Rumors snowball to the point where many were sure they were living in sin.

One elderly lady who didn't want to draw attention to herself however, she asked for prayer for Gregory, Jason, and Amber. She said, "with their parents living together in sin it must be hitting these little ones pretty hard." Pastor Palmer interrupted her and said, "yes sister Edna I think we get your point." The problem was the damage was already done.

Michael and Samantha were not really living together or having sex however, the truth was not as interesting as the rumors. As a result, one Sunday after church Michael announced to all his church family, "listen brothers and sisters. You call yourselves Christians. Yet, you are not acting like it! You are gossiping about my family and you don't know the truth. You tell a story about what you think is going on, a juicy story about what you would like there to be going on

but, it is just a bunch of garbage." Then he turned and looked at his beautiful girlfriend and said, "Samantha Rainer, I love you so much. I don't want to live any longer without you by my side. Will you do me the honor of becoming Mrs. Samantha Mitchell?" That she jumped up and said, "yes! I thought you'd never ask."

Discussion Questions

1. Does it really take guts to be a husband and father? What does it mean to be a godly man in the context of a family?

2. Is gossip sin? If so, why do we gossip? Do you gossip even in the slightest way? (Romans 1:29-32, Proverbs 12:18 and 16:27-28)

Chapter 3

Several Months Later

When Samantha and Michael got engaged it didn't stop any of the rumors like Michael hoped it would. It only made people more convinced that something was going on. If this wasn't bad enough a second faction was worried for Amber and Gregory. They loved each other and their relationship had become the metaphoric poster child for teen purity. So, this faction didn't want Michael and Samantha to be together for if their parents married the young lovers would be brother and sister and that was unacceptable.

Samantha and Michael had been engaged for only a few months now and they were very eager to get married. Even though many were against their union, they knew that they were doing the right thing at least, they thought they were. Although, their church felt that it would be weird if they got married, they were committed to St. Thomas Church and wanted Pastor Palmer to marry them.

It was not long after this time that they went to Pastor Palmer and officially announced their desire to get married. They said, "We know that we need premarital counseling, so when can we set that up?" Pastor Palmer said, "Are you doing anything this afternoon?" The couple said, "No, but of course we need to drop off our kids at home." Pastor Palmer told Michael and Samantha, "of course you will have a lot of issues to work out as a couple but during our first session of premarital counseling I want your whole family to come to talk about your issues as a blended family. Therefore, Pastor Palmer told them to bring the kids along. This meeting was right after the morning service and it was not going to be a short meeting so they ordered pizza.

They all went to the pastor's office. When they got there Steve told them to just sit and relax. Pastor Palmer asked Jason what he felt about his mom getting married and he just said offhandedly, "It's fine. Whatever makes mom happy." Pastor Palmer could tell Jason was trying to evade the question so he pushed a little harder and said, "come on Jason cut the pat answers I really want to know how you are feeling. Jason then replied, "You do not really want to hear from me and it is not going to make any difference what I have to say! You prudes think marriage is something so special, if it were, my dad would not have walked out on us!" Samantha then said, Jason, I love you and your sister so very much, and I do not want to say anything bad about your dad, but he made his choice. So, we need to move on." In disgust Jason said, "How can you be so flippant about moving on without dad? He was your husband, and our dad? But when another cute guy comes along you just forget about our father!" With these words of her son's, she broke down crying so heavily her words could scarcely be made out, "Jason it has been years. Your father is dead and you know it! He hurt me so horribly when he left and yes, I will always love your father but he is gone and he is not coming back!" Wiping her tears away she said, "Son you know how much we all miss him, nevertheless, we must move on with our lives."   He started out by asking the kids "what do you think about your parents getting married?" Gregory said, "I'm glad my dad found such a great lady to make him happy." Amber's reaction wasn't so positive. She said, " Michael is a great guy and it will be nice to have a dad, a guy... a guy who... who yeah, who won't be such a coward, and runs off on us!" By the time she said these words, she was sobbing so her mom and soon-to-be dad hugged her and tried to comfort her. Michael said, "Don't worry honey, I'll never leave. The only person more important to me than this family is God. I'm totally committed to this family so you can be assured I'm not leaving you and your brothers. "Then Amber let out a wail because the phrase, "your brothers" was like fingernails on a chalkboard to her.

After Amber calmed down, she said, "I love my mother and I can't wait for Michael to be my new stepdad but Michael is Gregory's dad, I love Gregory. I don't mean to be selfish but this will make my boyfriend like my brother. Eww gross!" The adults try to explain that Gregory would not be blood relation but that didn't help Amber feel much better. It didn't make much sense nevertheless, with her mom getting married and with the rumors it became too much for her. As a result, Amber expressed this to Gregory and she said, "I need to take a break from our relationship."

As the months progressed, the couple prepared to get married. It was a whirlwind of activity. The business of planning for the wedding and preparing to merge their lives was so hectic they didn't have time to think. All throughout this process they kept thinking "we forgot something but we can't figure out what it is" when they mentioned this to their pastor. The pastor asked "did you ask God if this is his will?" Michael said, "Well of course this is God's will. We both are single Christians and we are basically a family already." Pastor Palmer said, "That is all fine and good but, I said, did you ask God if this is his will?" Samantha interrupted the two men and said to her husband to be, "the answer would be no we need to remedy the situation right now." The couple grab their children and found a secluded spot telling their children, "We as a couple have made a mistake. You guys may have supported us but we never asked permission from God." Samantha prayed, "thank you Jesus for bringing this wonderful man into my life. After my husband walked out on me, I thought I wasn't worthy to be a wife. I love the children you gave me. I am willing to raise them on my own and if this marriage is not your will just say the word and I will call off the wedding. However, Lord Jesus I need your clear guidance. If this marriage is your will, allow me to be the help mate Michael needs. I want to honor and respect him as he is to honor and respect you." Then Michael prayed, "Jesus my lover and my friend I am not worthy to lead this family. You took from me, my beautiful wife Suzanna. I did not know how to raise the son you gave us without her. Now after all this time when Gregory is a man, you have given me a new family. Is Samantha the woman you have given me to love as my wife? Please bless my path. Give me the strength to do your will no matter how painful your Will might be in the short run. Help me to love and lead my bride and family as you love and lead your bride the church. In your name Lord Jesus amen."

Discussion Questions

1. Why do you need to invite God into your marriage?

2. If you are getting married and/or doing something else that you know is God honoring, why do you need to pray about what you're trying to do?

3. Can you go back and correct mistakes that you made? What mistakes do you need to correct?

4. (men) If we are head of our family what is wrong with not talking to your wife about important decisions? (women) What do you do when your husband (with good intentions forgets to talk to you about a big decision, that concerns your whole family? Ephesians 5:22-33

Chapter 4

The Present

Life is often like a roller coaster, just when you feel like you are on top and things could never get better, you end up in a valley. This is how things were for the Mitchell's. Everything seemed to be going well for this family however, as with Job the trials were bound to come.

Michael's architecture firm had just finished designing the plans for the tallest building in New New Deli. Now by big city standards The Joshua X Horn building wasn't anything special but, for the small city of New New Deli, Michigan this six Story office building that was (covered in mirrored glass) was eye-catching.

With his Twenty years of service to this firm, Michael thought he was a shoe in for a promotion. When Miss Shaw called him into her office. Marcy Shaw was a tall woman with blond hair. Michael had worked here long enough to know that look on his supervisor's face and it wasn't good. She always looks stern but when she had to fire people, she looked downright cold. It wasn't that she liked firing people. In fact, there was nothing she hated more about her job than laying people off but, with the bad economy buildings were not being built and orders were being canceled so Miss Shaw was told to lay off the highest-paid 1% of the staff. That meant Michael was on the chopping block.

His boss said, "The higher-ups in the firm have required me to make cutbacks. I love your creativity and the quality of your work. However, we simply cannot afford to keep you on at this firm so I am very sorry but, I have to let you go." I will however, most certainly give you a recommendation to whatever firm you apply at.

Samantha was at the doctor's office. Her doctor had ordered some test because she had come in complaining of a stomach flu that was bothering her after symptoms were holding on more than a week later. When the doctor came into the room he said, "There is nothing wrong, you and your baby will be just fine." Samantha was rather confused at first when she said, "huh? I'm over 40, I'm a little too old to be getting pregnant." Then he replied, "You may be a little too old but, you are pregnant." At hearing this, a sense of awe fell over her. She and her new husband were going to have a child of their own. This was going to be quite a surprise for her husband yet, she knew that Michael was going to be just as thrilled as she was. Something this big deserved to be a special occasion. She traded her night shift with another nurse and gave the kids money to go out for pizza. Unfortunately, not all surprises are good surprises Michael was on his way home with his bad news.

Michael came home earlier than Samantha had counted on yet, she was still glad to see him. She was still changing out of her work scrubs and into a lovely dress that she knew Michael enjoyed seeing her in. Michael on the other hand looked unusually depressed. When she came out of the bedroom and saw him looking so down, she asked, "Honey you look like you had a very hard day at work. Did something happen that you need to talk about?" Michael said in an angry tone, "yeah, something happened, I got laid off! Ms. Shaw said, she didn't want to fire me but with the merciless economy she had to let me go!"

At this point she wasn't so sure she wanted to share her good news. Because a baby would be one more bill they didn't need. But, how long should she keep their child from her husband and its father. As a result, she ripped the bandage off, even though she wanted to build up to it. She ended up blurting out, "we will be having a baby, I'm pregnant" At this point Michael fainted on the couch.

When he woke up, he said, "Did I hear you right? You're pregnant?" Samantha answered, "Yes!" so Michael nervously said, "okay? Cool?" He wasn't sure what to make out of this news. On one hand he was excited to have this wonderful product of Samantha's and his love, on the other hand it couldn't come at a worse time.

Michael was very depressed and felt worthless not knowing what to do. "My love, what am I supposed to do? Without a job, how can I support this family? If I can't support this family what good am I as a man?" mourned Michael. Samantha interrupted his pity party and said, "Listen here, Michael Mitchell, okay you don't have a job, so what? I am still a nurse. It is not like we don't have any money coming in. Besides, the man I married is a true son of God. He will trust his father to meet his and his family's needs and that man is you." Michael kissed his bride and said, "You are right beloved, now we should do, what we should have done in the first place, pray. 'Lord Jesus we are confused. I have lost this great paying job but at the same time you have blessed us with this baby. We have needs but we feel powerless to get those needs met."

Their prayer was interrupted by a call from their pastor. "hello" answered Michael." "Yes, this is Pastor Steve Palmer at the church. I was wondering if you knew of anyone who could use some work?" Michael replied, "Actually I need some work to do. I was just laid off this afternoon." Steve then asked, "Do you know how to do electrical work?" Michael reluctantly answered, "Funny you should ask that. I was trained by my father who was a certified electrician, to do electrical work, but I was more interested in architecture so I didn't go on to get my certification." Pastor Palmer said, "That shouldn't be a problem. Jim Samson is a licensed contractor and electrician he just needs a few workers so he was hoping to hire from the church. As you know with the growth, we have had in the youth department it has become a necessity to add on a youth wing to the building. So, are you up for it?" Michael didn't even need to think about it, for this job was an answer to his prayer.

The wing was basically a gym with an office/library for Pastor Brenda horn and her interns and a couple of classrooms. This job was really a blessing for Michael. Between looking for more permanent work and the work on the wing he did not have time to worry. Four months into the work Michael received a call from the hospital where his wife worked. "Are you Samantha Mitchell's husband?" He answered, "Yes" then they said, "You better get up here, your wife was spotting at work." So, Michael rushed to the hospital and when he got to his wife's room she was sobbing crouched up in the fetal position with slightly bloody feet. When she saw her husband, she cried out "we lost the baby! Why didn't I take it easier? As a middle-aged nurse I knew this pregnancy was going to be high risk." Michael wasn't sure of what to say so, he said, "we can try again." Samantha wasn't in the mood for these words that didn't help. Yet, she knew she had to cut him some slack, for he was a man and couldn't relate to what she was going through. So, she just said, "Just say nothing and hold me." That is what he did.

Jim Samson was very pleased with Michael's work on the youth wing. He knew that Michael was not a certified electrician but that it would not take much for him to get an apprenticeship that would lead to certification. So, Jim call his friend Berman Marrimaker about an apprenticeship for Michael in their electrical department of his factory. Before too very long Michael had a good paying job as an electrician at Marrimaker.

Discussion Questions

1. If we are seeking after God, will we face trouble? If so, why? (Mathew 10:24, Luke 22:27, John 13:16, John 15:20, 2 Timothy 3:12)

2. Why would God let us go through such pain if he loves us? (Romans 8:28, Ephesians 6:4)

3. When bad things like layoffs happen how can we be sure that God meets our needs? (Luke 12:6-7)

4. Are you worthless if you cannot fulfil your traditional roles (i.e.: a man without a job/ a woman unable to give birth)? Phil. 1:6, Palms 139:5-6, 13-16

Chapter 5

Ten Years Ago

Brenda horn grew up in a very traditional home. It was a good home where she knew she was loved. If she had any complaints, it was that gender roles were too well established. Her father worked outside the home to support the family, while her mother stayed at home to take care of the domestic tasks. When she said that she felt a calling to the ministry her parents accused her of using God's name in vain. Her father said, "Young lady St. Paul clearly stated in 1 Corinthians 14:34* 'let your women keep silent in the church, for they are not permitted to speak; but they are to be submissive, as the law also says." In short Brenda knew her parents felt she was sinning, wanting to be a pastor yet she knew her calling and it was to be a pastor.

Ten Years Later

She enjoyed working with teenagers and the only pastoral major her Bible college offered to women was children and youth ministry. So, after college she became a youth pastor. She hadn't even tested her wings out when she found an assignment at a small church, in the small town of Hartlin, Michigan. This church was a little more modern than what she was used to yet, not so much that she felt uncomfortable.

Brenda was a very intelligent and organize person. however, the way she organized things show just how much she believed in the saying, "If you want something done right, you got to do it yourself." For the first little while she kept the number of teens attending the group steady. As time went on the youth group lost more and more people. Until all that was left was the children of the core members.

Pastor Palmer called her into his office one day and said, "Ms. Horn, I'm worried about how things are going with the youth group. I do understand that you want the teens to be well biblically educated, this is very good. However, it is driving away the less mature believers and seekers. Yet, you are doing nothing in terms of outreach." Then he said, "one easy thing you can do it since you have trained your teens so well. How about you do some outreach projects with them." Well, Brenda didn't take this well to say the least.

She talked to a former professor of hers from college, about what to do about the situation. This professor of hers told her, "Steven Palmer is your lead pastor, like it or not he is the boss. In addition, to that he is right. Remember how I talk about type A and type B personalities? You are a classic type A personality. Everybody who knows you can see you are type A. You are terrified to delegate responsibility. Yet, I promise if you let the teens participate in their group it will grow like a weed and you will not be so stressed out."

She like the idea but it sounded too good to be true. Could she just handover control to those students? Brenda was nervous about doing this and to be honest wasn't even sure in what way her teens could have an active role in their youth ministry. So, she sought out advice of one of the youth pastors of New New Deli Wesleyan Church. She truly loathed going to them for advice but, they were very generous with their help. Many of her former students left her group for theirs.

Brenda asked, "Why did my students leave my group for yours? What are you doing that I am not?" Mel and Carol Lever, the youth pastors she talked to said, "Well we don't know what you do. However, as for us we just try to be genuine with the teens. We love our teens with the love of God." Then Brenda said, "Well of course we have to love teenagers. We wouldn't be in the youth ministry if we didn't care about teens." The Levers said, "well don't just care about these kids, because you don't want them to go to hell. As the Bible says, "While we were yet sinners Christ died for us, to us that is our duty. So even if our teens don't have any interest in knowing God right now, we need to give them all that we have in the hopes that they will one day know the one that will never leave them, Jesus Christ our friend and lover. Sometimes it breaks our hearts to see our students get pregnant or getting involved with some other self-destructive activities but, we love each of them like we would our own children." The statement left Brenda speechless, for she knew that she certainly wasn't loving Jason when she called him the Devil. Afterward she said,

"My mentor said I should let the students have a part in the ministry. How do I do this?" Carol said, "At our church the teens lead the worship for the youth ministry and we help the teens find ways to use their gifts and talents to serve God. Some of the teens even lead small groups."

Brenda had tried these things with her group it didn't go quite as well as she hoped for and she had to let go of her ego and need for control. Her group was so small that some of the activities that the students may have wished to do couldn't be done yet, other things they were able to do with some modification. One student played the guitar others took turns teaching the lesson (with Preapproval of the lessons.) The group grew to the point where within a year Brenda was forced to ask the church board for use of the sanctuary on Wednesday nights for a youth service and it continued to grow. The youth program grew so big that it outnumbered the rest of the church four to one, as a result St. Thomas Church decided to build a new youth wing to help the group to be able to continue to grow.

Discussion Questions

1. What is the purpose of gender roles? Are they important? If so why or why not?

2. How do you balanced outreach to the lost, giving spiritual milk to new believers and meat to the spiritually mature?

3. What benefit do believers get from participating in ministry? (Matthew 10)

4. What attitude should you have to be in effective minister? (Luke 14:25-35, John 8:1-11)

5. Are you really willing to give your time, resources, and life so that those around you can have a relationship with Jesus?

6. Why do we need to encourage people to use their gifts (1 Corinthians 12)? Why do we feel so good when we are using our gifts?

Chapter 6

Terminology

Neurodivergent: Differing in mental or neurological function from what is considered typical or normal (frequently used with reference to autistic spectrum disorders); not neurotypical Neurotypical: not displaying or characterized by autistic or other neurologically atypical patterns of thought or behavior:

Autism: a pervasive developmental disorder that commonly manifests in early childhood, characterized by impaired communication, excessive rigidity, and emotional detachment: now considered one of the autism spectrum disorders.

Definitions are from Dictionary.com

A Few Months Earlier

Brenda Horn was awoken bright and early, by a call on her day off. She found this odd since she was not use to people calling her at 8a.m. on a Monday morning. Even, telemarketers rarely called her at that time but, since she did not recognize the phone number, she let it go to voicemail. When she listened to the message, she was surprised to discover it was not a solicitor but a student from Indiana Wesleyan University looking for an internship. The student said, "Hello, Miss Horn my name is Jimmy Van York. My Young Adult Pastor, Gabriel Jordan, said I should call you, he said he knew you, and that you are a great person to learn from. I am looking for an internship." At first, Brenda did not know what to make of this but she had to admit an intern would take some pressure off her shoulders. Therefore, she called him back. She said, ok, when can you come in for an interview. He said, "I will be coming home for the weekend in two weeks, can we do an interview sometime that Friday?" She was used to being the one to set the date of appointments like this, but she agreed to the time and date. She had a background check done on James Van York, and she talked to Jimmy's pastor. A man Brenda knew very well from college. They had been close friends. Gabriel said, "Jimmy would make a wonderful addition to your ministry staff still, he has some weaknesses that you should ask about because, they are not my business to talk about. That statement made Brenda more than a little suspicious about what this weakness could be.

Jimmy was well prepared for his interview. He had references, his portfolio was ready to present. Anything an Interviewer could ask for, he had it ready to offer. Jimmy had superb answers for all of Brenda's questions. He almost seemed to be too good to be true. The only that gave her pause was the fact that he would not look at her. She tried to dismiss it as him just being nervous. However, Gabriel's statement about a weakness left her haunted, wondering, "what it could be?" Could it be something that threatened to her newly thriving youth ministry?

She then the question everyone feared "What is your greatest weakness?" With a deep breath, Jimmy said, "Well I do not think of it as a weakness per say nevertheless you might call it that. I have Asperger's Syndrome." Brenda had heard the phrase spoken a lot but didn't really know what it was so, she asked, "what it was and how it would affect his ministry?" Jimmy said, it is an autism spectrum disorder. At that Brenda mockingly said, "What how can you have autism? Isn't that some intellectual disorder? You are clearly a very bright young man." Jimmy who was extremely offended at this point took another deep breath and said, "Ms. Horn yes, I am a very intelligent person and so are many other famous autistics like Dan Aykroyd and Albert Einstein. Autism takes many forms that is why we call it a spectrum. My form of autism is call Asperger's Syndrome which to put it in basic terms causes me to act in ways some people find eccentric in social situations. I have sensory issues so when we are doing activities that are on the loud side, I will be wearing ear plugs and I do not like bright light so I will be the first to put on sun glasses. Also, as you may have noticed I am uncomfortable looking people in the eye."

Brenda did not have a problem with his sensory issues yet, what caused her some concern was the idea that Asperger's was a social disorder. This worried her because so much of youth ministry was social. So, she asked, how he would function in this group with it being so much about the social interaction with the teens. He said, "I like being around people but like most people I gravitate more so to people like myself. Therefore, I will be a benefit because I can 34 reach those that otherwise may fall through the cracks, since they likely do not fit in with the rest of the group. There was just one more question Brenda and (Pastor Palmer was also there) had for Jimmy. "Where will you be living this summer?" He said, "With my folks" I'm from the unincorporated community of Spittle. Spittle is only a 45 minutes' drive from Hartlin. So, they agreed to let him be a youth ministry intern.

Jimmy was one of Brenda's first intern therefore, initially, she was not sure what to have him do. However, as the summer went on, she found increasingly more for him to do. When the teens needed a driver to different outings, he did that. Nevertheless, there were bumps along the road.

On the very first Friday night of the summer the teens had a gym night. He had to chaperon the event. Now actually Brenda assumed that since he was a guy, he would enjoy the gym night. In reality, athletics was a drudgery to Jimmy but, he made the best of it. He watched them and when one of the guys asked him to play basketball with them, he played yet, he was very awkward and he tripped and fell several times. When he could find people to play fewer physical games such as, foosball or chess with, he did that. Then a few weeks later it was time for Big Ticket Festival (a Christian Music Festival in Gaylord, MI) and he was looking forward to this event. Ever since, he heard he may be back in Michigan and that the youth group was going he had saved up his money. Despite this, he knew that this festival would be rough on him therefore he packed plenty of ear plugs and a good pair of sunglasses, along with the usual supplies.

The next week was a slower more normal week. One day while taking a brief break from writing the lesson for the upcoming youth service she took a walk around the youth wing. She noticed the wing sounded too quiet. "Didn't I see Jimmy this morning? Where is that intern of mine anyway?" She thought to herself. It was not just that the wing was silent that, caused her to wonder if Jimmy was in the building. The lights were off in the intern office. Since he was the only intern that summer, he could get away with shutting the lights off. She went to the office and looked in. Jimmy was there working on the project Brenda had given him that morning. He was working by the dim light of a small lamp on the table. When he saw her, he said, "Yes, Ms. Horn what can I do to help you?" She answered, "Nothing, I was just surprised to see the lights were off in here. I was beginning to wonder if you were even in the building." Jimmy said, "after such a busy sensory filled week I very much needed to recover and this is how I de-stress. If I do not, I am may have a melt-down." "Cool" She replied, as she was leaving Jimmy stopped her and said, "While I have your attention I was wondering if I will have a chance to give the lesson sometime during the youth service?" She said, "Well I had not thought about it. But, if you have a lesson ready you could give it in the service a week from this coming Wednesday." At hearing that he said, "that's great I will have a wonderful lesson ready to go!"

The Wednesday that he was to give his youth message he was nervous yet, not as nervous as he looked. He always paced and talked to himself however few people really noticed until now because he had been working in the background. Now that he would be teaching the lesson for the night, he was up front. Some of the teens thought he looked a little odd yet, as soon as he started speaking these young people were mesmerized. Brenda Horn was very knowledgeable about scripture; Jimmy was knowledgeable about scripture and could present God's word in a dramatic way that kept their attention and wetted their appetite to learn even more. After the success, Jimmy had Brenda decided Jimmy should do the preaching regularly. You would have thought that no one would have wanted to let him go. Although, that was not the case.

There were many adults including many of the parents that were uncomfortable with Jimmy because of his peculiar behavior. A few were so unnerved by the way he acted and they asked to have him dismissed as an intern. Brenda stuck up for Jimmy and convinced the board to allow him to finish out his internship. However, Brenda had been so impressed by Jimmy that, she was hoping to offer him an assistant youth pastor position (after he graduated from college.) Now the best she could do was give him a glowing recommendation. After this incident she informed Jimmy about what happened but let him know that he would be able to finish the summer out and that she was impressed by what a fine minister he was. This shook him up nevertheless he finished the summer out strong.

Note From Author

The Church is a family of chosen sons and daughters of God. Each and every one of us have strengths and weaknesses. I am a child of God, and I am autistic. We, like all of God's image bearers are not a mistake. We have a lot to offer the Church but, we are not always sure what we have to offer. At the same time there are some simple things the Church can do to help us and, others with similar issues.

There is a saying, "you met one autistic person, you met one autistic person." We are all very different but, what I am about to say is true for many of us.

In general, we autistic people have sensory issues which basically means sometimes we are overly sensitive to sensory input other times we may be under sensitive. This causes what some perceive as "odd behavior." Which causes people to be uncomfortable around us. All we are asking is for you to understand that sensory overload is painful for us. So how does this effect the ministry of the church.

First, greeters may make your neural typical visitors feel welcome however, they are no friend to us and they make us feel uncomfortable. One autistic person I talked to, referred to getting passed the greeters as "running the gauntlet." This really is an apt description of what it feels like to enter a church with greeters even, if it is your own church and even more so, if you are a visitor. An autistic believer just wants to worship God without being bothered by a greeter. So how can you keep from making others feel uncomfortable while, still being welcoming. The greeters can move back a little bit. Having greeters right at the door feels very claustrophobic although, if the greeters were just a little bit farther inside those who do not wish to be greeted can avoid the greeters without making visitors who do wish to be greeted feel noticed.

Then there are things that are considered normal and enjoyable to neural typicals (NTs) that is not comfortable and/ or normal to some of us. As a result, our reaction might seem standoffish maybe even rude to NTs. There is the ritual of greeting other people at church by shaking hands some autistics like myself are not comfortable doing this. I prefer to give a firm head nod. Others choose to walk out during this time. We come to church to worship God not to shake people's hands. Now some of us don't have a problem with shaking hands but if you notice that one of us is uncomfortable doing this please do not take offense.

Next, this is not an issue for me however, it can be an issue for some, the noise. Of course, if it becomes too big of issue, they can find a different church. Nevertheless, there is something you can do to help these who just need it to be, a little quieter. Some churches have installed one or more closed circuit TVs in the lobby. Where people that are not able to be in the sanctuary for one reason or another can watch the service. This maybe just enough for some of us.

In addition, to these, other sensory inputs can be bothersome. Most of this can be dealt with by just having awareness and common courtesy. For example, perfumes and other fragrances can be annoying to others around you including, autistic people. Therefore, please avoid wearing them to church.

Another form of sensory input that can to varying degree be tormenting is bright light. It is true that some people use sunglasses for fashion and if someone is solely using them for this purpose that can be rather disrespectful. However, for an autistic person if it is overly bright inside or outside, they are needed.

Many autistic people have a great deal of difficulty when it comes to social interaction with NTs. For us social interaction is like an English speaker going over to a part of Japan where no body speaks English. You can learn to speak Japanese conversationally. Nevertheless, there could still be subtleties that native speakers likely know naturally yet, you as a foreigner may struggle to understand. This is a big reason some of us do not enjoy doing some of the more public activities in the church.

So, what does the autistic community have to offer the church? Like every Child of God, we have been given gifts and talents. But in general, autistic people tend to be rather detail oriented as well as having particularly good artistic and/or analytical minds. Right now, in some church there may be an autistic woman who everybody in her church has overlooked but God has given her great skill at composing music and if given the chance she possibly has already written a lovely worship song that completely expresses what God has been doing with her church body in the last year. At another local church there is an autistic man who is very quiet and never says a word but understands numbers like a calculator. If given the chance this man might be the very best treasurer his church has ever had. He can stretch every penny so far, that not only will he be able to find a way for his church to buy the sound system that they have been saving up for (without going into debt) he has found a way to afford to pay the man whose, family just started attending this church, to install the system. As a result, this family can eat another week.

Some other not so public ministries that we can do are: bring deserts, be a prayer warrior, tech person/ tech team, A/V operator, pastoral research aid, janitor. However, like all people if the LORD calls us to do something even if it makes us uncomfortable, we must do it.   "(Jesus') grace is enough for you. When you are weak, (his) power is made perfect in you." So (you will be) very happy to brag about (your) weaknesses. Then Christ's power can live in (you). (2 Corinthians 12:9, New Century Version)

Discussion Questions

1. Do you judge people simply by their appearance? If so, why?

2. Why is it wrong to judge people by their appearance?   1 Corinthians 12:22-26

3. Is it vital for a male youth worker to be a macho, super athlete? Why might parents object to an intern that does not demonstrate these traits?

4. How might an Asperger's Syndrome person relate better to some youth?

5. What does it mean to accept, or understand an autistic? Should everyone else in the church be burdened just to accommodate one staff member?

Chapter 7

Present Day

Mrs. Edna Clyne is an elderly widow. She has walked with the lord for as long as she can remember. Consequently, she is as old fashioned as they come.

She loved her husband George and their child. Her husband has been dead for many years, Yet, she never remarried. Therefore, she has become quite comfortable and set in her ways.

One day two of her youngest grandkids, Annie and her brother Billy came to visit for the week. They normally live in Mundy Township so they don't get to see their grandmother very often. Like many children, they were full of energy and very joyous. As they were riding to their grandma's house, their parents said, "Now children, remember to be respectful. Your grandma is older, she loves you and is due honor." Then their father said, "If she uses a word or two that you know should not be used, let it go. We can talk about it on the way home if we must." When they reached Edna's house she was waiting for them on her porch. Edna asked her son Micah and her daughter-in-law Esther, "how was the drive up here?" Micah answered, "it was ok but it was a long drive." Edna responded, "I can tell." She was referring to the fact that her grandkids were running around chasing each other. However, she was prepared for this. Edna had lunch ready for the family. She fixed hotdogs so the family could eat outside if the kids couldn't sit still.

Edna let her daughter-in-law know when she was ready for the kids to eat. It was her way of saying "Mother; control those kids of yours!" and get everyone to come and eat. As soon as Micah finished praying, the kids began scarfing down food. When Edna looked at her grandkids she couldn't help thinking, "has anyone taught these kids manners?" after Annie and Billy finished eating, they washed their hands and faces. Then, they asked if they could go play. Their parents said, "If it's okay with your grandmother." Edna said, "Just go play."

After Annie and Billy's parents left, Billy noticed that a family was moving in next door to their grandma. It was a young family with a boy who appeared to be around their age. The kids ran to tell their grandma. "Grandma, Grandma, a family is moving next door and they have a child about our age!" Edna told her grandkids "Kids, Kids, don't bug the neighbors!" The children said, "We won't!" and they went off running.

Annie tried to introduce herself and her brother, "Hello! I'm Annie and this is my little brother Billy. I see you have a son about our age." When their grandma caught up to them, she scolded them saying "Billy, Annie don't you know better than to talk to strangers!" "Well weren't you going to welcome them to the neighborhood?" replied the kids. Edna thought to herself, "No I wasn't planning on it."

The wife and mother who moved in said, "We don't mind, in fact we were hoping that our son Jerome could meet some friends fairly quickly." Then she introduced her husband and herself to Edna. "This is my Husband Jared and I'm Joann Redding." Jared stuck his hand out to shake hands with his new neighbor, but Edna was nervous about shaking hands with a black man. She didn't want to be rude so she went with it. Jared could sense Edna's discomfort so he tried to wrap up the conversation. His wife, who wasn't perceptive and much more of a people person said, "Hey we just moved here from Chicago and we have been going to a mega church there. So, we need to find a new church here." Edna said, "I don't know of any fancy mega churches around here. As far as I know, most of the churches around here are like my church, St. Thomas Church. They are small and traditional. Joann said, "Great, sounds like a great place to check out first." Jared sensing Edna's desire to go but not be rude said, "It was nice to meet you. Hope to get to know you better in the future."

Edna was glad to get out of there. For this interracial family made her very uncomfortable, in fact, they made her more than uncomfortable. Edna would not admit this to herself or anyone else. Edna saw this family as a mistake, a pollution of the white race.

The kids were surprised when their grandma hurried them and herself away from the neighbor's house. They asked, "Grandma, why did we leave so soon? We wanted to play with Jerome." "Children didn't you see they were busy moving in?" asked their grandmother. Then Billy and Annie said, "Ok, but couldn't we at least set up a play date?" Edna sighed, "You stubborn kids. If you must know, it's because I don't want you to associate with those mongrels." This statement confused the grandchildren so Billy said, "Grandma, you are funny. Jarome is a boy not a doggy." Edna said while trying to change the subject, "children you are too young to understand. What do you want to do tomorrow?"

Annie felt that the subject was unsettled but she knew as her parents had said to respect her grandma no matter how odd the situation was so she said, "How about we go swimming at the beach?" their grandmother said, "That sounds great!" Billy said, "I don't care what we do but sometime this week I want to play with Jerome!" His sister looked at him as to say "Billy no" Edna told her grandson "We'll see" but what she really meant was "I don't think so kid."

Edna took her grandkids to a beach off Lake Michigan. The water was cold but the kids had fun nevertheless. There were dunes near this beach so they pretended to be thirsty travelers, dying in the Sahara Desert. Edna took pictures. They all had a great time. It was a day they never wanted to end.

Early Sunday morning, Joann woke up her husband and son. Jared had warned his wife that they might not be welcome at this white redneck church. But Joann dismissed him saying, "Nonsense you worry wart, I grew up in a traditional white church. It might be different than our old church but I'm sure we'll fit right in." Jerome who had gone to the same church all his life asked, "Why do we have to get up so early momma?" Then she told him about Sunday school which sparked his curiosity.

When they walked in the door, Jared commented to his wife that he felt a little underdressed since everyone was in their best dress clothes but no one seemed to notice how casually dressed they looked. The moment the Redding's walked into the church, they were treated like guests of honor. St. Thomas Church rarely got visitors, so for them to get a visitor was a special occasion and they wanted to make sure they felt welcome.

When Edna saw the Redding's at her church, she thought to herself, "they showed up, can't they see this is a white church?" On the other hand, Annie and Billy were excited to see Jerome. When they saw Jerome, they grabbed his hand and the children ran to their class. But, before they could get too far, their grandmother scolded them. "Annie, Billy! Don't run in church!"

During the service, the children were rather hyper because they were bored but to Edna's surprise Jerome was more respectful. "Did you remember your change for the offering? Don't you want to be rich?" Said Edna, to her grandchildren. Their parents explained to them that getting rich is not the reason to give but out of the love for God. However, their grandma believed people should give to God, so that God will bless them. She always quoted Luke 6:30 'give and it will be given to you' good measure, pressed down, shaken together, and running over will be put into your bosom. For with the same measure you use, it will be measured back to you.' (NKJV)

Pastor Palmer preached from John 17:20-26 about how god's desire was that all believers are supposed to act as one in Christ. Edna thought it was a very good sermon. But she didn't see 43 how it applied to her. On the way home Edna turned on the car radio to her favorite radio preacher Rev. Bubba J.T. Barns and this is what she heard. "In genesis 'And the lord formed man out of the dust of ground, and breathed into his nostrils the breath of life; and man became a living being. But, for Adam there was not found a helper comparable to him. And the Lord God caused a deep sleep to fall upon Adam, and he slept and took one of his ribs, and closed up the flesh in its place. Then the rib which the Lord God had taken from man he made into a woman, and he brought her to the man. (Genesis 2:7&206-22, NKJV) Listen to me brothers and sisters, does this say God created Juan and Maria,

Lee and Sue Lee, Jerome and Mowesa? NO! Despite what some of us have been taught as children, the black man who fixes your car is as much your brother as your white mailman! All people black, white, Asian, Hispanic, Native American or whatever all came from our same first parents, Adam, and Eve. So, we have no reason to look down on or be prejudice against anyone!

Edna at this point was realizing she hadn't heard a word from her grand kids in a while so she wondered what was up and she realized they had fallen asleep. Edna didn't want to listen and God knew it so he caused the children to fall asleep so he can get Edna's full undivided attention. God spoke and said, "Edna, Edna listen to me. I know you were taught that ethnic groups shouldn't mix. Well, I never said this. I created all people in my image. I personally painted the human race with all the paints in my pallet and, they are all beautiful to me. Who are you to say the races shouldn't mix? If I chose to combine color, then I chose it. If someone chooses me as their Lord, they are my child. STOP your secret hatred of the Redding family. I love them just as much as I love you."

It was hard for Edna to swallow this. She didn't want to believe it was God speaking but, it clearly was. She had no choice but to listen and obey. So, she said, "Lord, if this is you speaking, I must obey. Yet, how? How do I get over a mindset that has become core to me?" God said, "just trust me. I can do anything and, I will help you where you are weak."

Just as Edna and her grandchildren pulled into the driveway, Annie and Billy woke up. Edna never liked to do a lot of cooking on the Lord's Day so they had sandwiches. Then she said to her grand kids, "who wants to go over to the Redding's house?" Billy and Annie were very excited because they were eager to see Jerome so they said, "I do, I do!" the three of them walked over to the Redding's house. Edna, of course wasn't as excited as the kids were to see the neighbors. But she swallowed her pride and knocked on the Redding's door. Joann answered the door wearing a frilly apron that looked like something from a 50's sitcom. She said, "Edna, it is so nice to see you. I just threw in my grandma's pineapple upside down cake, God bless her soul. If you can stay a while, I would love to have you try some."

In the distance the two women heard Jared saying something but could not make it out. Joann said to her husband, "Oh hush hun!" Edna said, "What was your husband saying?" Joann said, "oh its nothing. He just has this crazy idea that you don't like us because we are an interracial family. Isn't that crazy?" Edna said, "Madam, you should respect your husband and not dismiss his discernment so quickly. To be honest he is right. I was being racist and I came to apologize. I was raised to believe white people and colored people should never mix. However, God has been showing me the error of my ways." Joann responded, "Mrs. Clyne thank you for the apology." Jarod who had made it to the door by this time said, "I am glad that you are able to admit your mistakes. I know it must not be easy for you."

Edna then said, "I can't promise that I have completely changed but, I will do my best to see you as a Christian family and not as a bunch of race mixers." Jared said, "I wasn't expecting you to change your mind in only a few hours. Your honesty only makes me respect you more."

Edna and the Redding's kept talking and getting to know each other, while the kids played. Throughout the rest of the week Annie and Billy played with Jerome quite often. When their parents picked them up, Annie and Billy bragged about all the fun they had, had

Discussion Questions

1. Do you have a prejudice that keeps you from interacting with people you need to associate with?

2. How do you overcome learned core beliefs that are wrong? (Acts 10:9-48)

3. Does God really talk to people? If he does, how do we know it is him talking to us? (1 John 4:1, Exodus 15:26)

4. Wives, how are you doing on respecting your husbands? How can you best show respect to your husbands? Husbands, how are you doing on loving your wives? How can you best show love to your wives? (1 Corinthians 7)

5. What should be our motive for giving?

Chapter 8

The Following School Year

Joann Redding had moved with her family to Hartlin, Michigan to work as an assistant head-start teacher. She had just graduated that past summer and she was eager to start teaching preschoolers. Her lead teacher was impressed with how well she related to both the children and their parents. To her surprise her classroom was inside of her church, St. Thomas Church.

One day a mother named Zoey Meijers, came to pick up her son. Ms. Meijers tried to hide it but, Joann could read it on her face, Ms. Meijers was wore out. She knew from experience that being a mother of a young child was not easy, yet, Zoey looked more than the normal amount of fatigue Joann was used to seeing in the parents of her students.

Joann said, "Mrs. Meijers you look dead tired is anything wrong?" Zoey said, "the same old same old. I work full-time and raise Max full-time with no breaks and no family to help me" Throwing her hands up in frustration "I feel like I am going to explode!". Joann said, "It was not that long ago I was raising my own ball of energy and going to college at the same time. Now I will admit unlike you I technically had family around but I might as well say, that I did not. My husband worked to support my education. So, when I saw him my mind was pretty much asleep and I could not appreciate his help with Jerome (our child). About the only thing that helped me keep my sanity was my friends at my M.O.P.S. groups. Joann could see the glazed over look on Zoey's face so Joann explained that M.O.P.S. stands for mothers of preschoolers. Zoey at this point was anxious to get home and fix dinner for her son and herself so she said, "Sound like fun but, I can't, I need to get home and fix dinner for Max and myself"

Joann then said, "There will be an M.O.P.S. meeting across the hall in a half hour. Ms. Meijers you need this. You do not need to worry about getting home to fix dinner. Connie Miller is one of those super mom's that puts all of us to shame. She will be bringing her addictive lasagna. Please Don't think coming commits you to do more work there are a hand full of moms in the group who love making dishes to pass I have learned to just let them make everybody's life easier. Just leave Max here and enjoy the group. We will make sure he gets fed." Zoey felt pressured to come to this mommy's group but she thought "whatever, it's a break from my bratty son." Then she felt guilty for thinking of her child in that way.

As the meeting went on some of the mothers seemed to have everything together. Yet, she discovered many of the women in this group were struggling to be good moms even the stay-at-home-mothers. Now there were things that seemed a little hokey like the crafts. She just was not a crafty person. However, other things were very helpful. Most importantly the time she got to be herself without being on the clock.

One of the mothers introduced herself to Zoey, "Hey, my name is Naomi. Do you attend this church because I don't remember ever seeing you?" Zoey said, "I have never been inside a Church except, to take my son to preschool." Zoey asked, "Does it matter?" Naomi replied, "Nah, but you should check this church out. For such a small congregation, they have a wonderful children's program." Zoey then said, "I really cannot afford my son's babysitter. There is no way I can afford one more bill." Zoey said this because she did not know that the kids' program at church was free. Zoey's comment confused Naomi for a moment then, she laughed it off as a bad joke and said, "the children's program is free, and I think your son will have a fantastic time." Trying to get out of this conversation Zoey said, "I work most Sundays but if I have a free one, I certainly should try attending this church. Oh, what is a congregation?" When Zoey said, she had never gone to church she meant it. Naomi did not expect this question so she just said, "you know the people that attend the church on a Sunday." Naomi tried to be nice with her answer but it still left Zoey feeling embarrassed that she did not know things that were second nature to these women. Zoey's grandmother was the last member of her family that may have step through the doors of a church building and Zoey was not even sure if she (her grandmother) ever attended Church. So, Christiane see terms like congregation and saved were a foreign language to Zoey. After the meeting, Zoey picked her son up and they went home. Joann asked Zoey what she thought of M.O.P.S.? Zoey said, "It was ok. However, I'm not a crafty person. I don't have the room and time to take care of 'pretty things?'" Joann said, "I totally get it, I'm not a crafter myself. That is the way they relax. Me I'd rather just go for a walk and enjoy the sights and sounds of nature." "I have not had a moment of just plain relaxation since before I got knocked up," replied Zoey. Joann responded; I would love to babysit Max for free. When Zoey heard this she couldn't help but wonder what this lady's motive was, because she sure seemed eager to get her hands on her (Zoey) kid. You need some time to relax, it is not good for you to keep going without sometime to de-stress." Then Joann handed Zoey her home phone number. Zoey said, "I just might take you up on your offer. See you on Monday."

Very early Sunday morning Max jumped on his mother's bed and said, "Wake up momma!" "What's wrong baby?" responded Zoey who was still half asleep. Her son replied, "Mama you gotta get up! Nicky says that today they do this thing called Sunday School at my school! (which is at St. Thomas Church) They play games and hear stories. It sounds like so much fun." Zoey did not want to get up but, her son kept persisting and shaking her covers so after some time she relented and got up, fixed breakfast, and got ready to go to church. There was only one problem and, it was a big one. Neither of them were sure when church started.

They did the only thing they could do they drove to the church to find out when everything started. When Zoey got there the sign said" Sunday School—10:00a.m. Worship—11:00a.m. Evening 6:00p.m.

Wednesday 7:00p.m. It was 9a.m. She told her son, "they are not open Max and you don't want to wait do you?" Max said, "Mamma you did not even try the door." So, she said, "fine I will try the door" and so her son and her walked over and tried the front door of the church.

When they did, the door was unlocked but not all the lights were on and she could not see anyone around so, Zoey wondered if they were even supposed to be here. They walked into a large room and found Mrs. Redding squatting in front of what looked like a short wall around the stage. Zoey tapped Joann on the back and said, "ahh, Joann what is going on and are we supposed to be here?" Joann replied, "Ms. Meijers I am so happy to see you here today. I felt like God was telling me that I needed to come into church early this morning and pray at the altar. Brenda the youth pastor let me in." Zoey asked, "What is an altar?" Joann answers this wall is called the altar. Zoey said, "hope you do not mind me asking these questions. I am sure I sound stupid asking questions that are probably very common sense to you. It's just I was not raised in the church. I think my grandmother maybe went to church but, I am not even sure about that. Joann said, "I do not think you are stupid. I am glad you are curious and asking." To be honest she was not even sure why she was curious. Because even though one part of herself was curious, every other part said, "this is weird and I want to take my kid and get as far away from here as I can." Joann said, "I am a Sunday school teacher for the early elementary children's class but we have time to talk so please come with me.

My son Jarome is in the gym playing so Max can play with him while we talk." Zoey said, "what do you want to talk to me about?" Joann said, "whatever you want to talk about I'm game." Zoey asked, "What is up with you church people? Is this just a social club for goody two shoes like the YMCA or the Lions Club? Because I ain't no goody two shoes I'm just a mom." Joann replied, "You know so am I. Nobody is perfect and God knows it, that is why Jesus came to Earth." Zoey asked is that the Baby I see in the Christmas decorations? Joann answered, "yes" then she went on to explain that the Bible, which is God's Love letter and instruction book for us humans says, we all have disobeyed God's wishes since God's standard is perfection we are headed for Hell." Zoey interrupted, "How the Hell am I supposed to know what God wants, that is not fair!" Joann said, "Jesus who is God told us what God wants from us, He wants us to 'Love the Lord your God with all your heart and with all your soul and with all your mind. And the second is like it: 'Love your neighbor as yourself.' (Matthew 22:37, 39*)

Zoey said, "that sounds simple enough, don't we all do that?" Joann said, "have you ever in your whole life lied to anyone?" Zoey answered of course I have. Who has not?" "Jesus has not because lying is sin or displeasing God. However, God loved us so much he put on human skin and lived as a human and died by us the very people he came to save," replied Joann. Now Zoey was more confused than ever, so she asked, "Why would you kill Jesus if he is your God?" Joann answered, "Jesus took on all the sins of every person that ever lived when he died so, anytime you have sinned you have killed Jesus." Zoey then asked, "If Jesus is dead, why do you worship Him. A dead God cannot be much of a God?" Joann replied "I worship him because he proved he is God by rising from the dead. But I need to go to my Sunday school class now. Follow me and I will show you to an adult class I think you will like, we can talk after church." The two women and their children went to their respective classes.

Everyone in Zoey's class was very nice nevertheless, even here there were issues. The teacher had people look up verses in the Bible. But she had no idea how to find the passages, people were talking about. She saw names like: Matthew, Luke, and Romans. Also, she saw that there were big numbers and little numbers yet, she was not sure how they worked together. Therefore, out of embarrassment she remained silent.

Joann did not realize just how confused and uncomfortable things would be for Zoey still, she did recognize that Zoey would be somewhat lost so she told her friend that she would pick her up after the class and walk her to the sanctuary. Zoey went with it however; she was extremely anxious after sitting through a class that made little sense to her. Joann could tell Zoey was very uncomfortable so she said, "Zoey you look nervous what is wrong?" Zoey said, "I am so lost I just have no idea what is going on. It feels like everyone is speaking a foreign language and I just can't figure out what anyone is saying. I took one of those papers the greeter was giving out (bulletins) and it has a lot more words that make no sense to me." So, Joann said, "This has been too much for you, hasn't it?" Zoey said, "Yes!" Joann then asked, "You mind if we get out of here, my family and I will take you and your son out for pizza," Zoe said, "That is very nice but unexpected of you."

The Redding family took Zoey and her son out for Pizza. Max was excited because he rarely if ever was able to have take-out pizza. While they waited for the pizza to come Jared thanked "God for their lunch, "LORD Jesus you are such a great provider. You are the giver of all things. We confess we do not always appreciate what you bring into our lives but you are our loving Father and you work all things out for your good. Thank you for letting us meet the Meijer's family and let them know how much you love them. In your name, Amen." Once Zoey knew Jared Redding was done praying, she asked, "aren't you ever embarrassed to pray in public like this" and he said, "No, why should I. He's the one I want to build my life around. I don't care what other people think of me when I pray in public. Yet, I also try not to make my prayers a spectacle. Prayer is just talking to God."

Joann then said, "Today you asked me to explain to you what the Hymn 'Washed in the blood of the lamb' was about. Well, as I told you we all have done things that displease God. Now the surprising thing is before God created the world, he knew that we would sin. Yet, he still chose to create the world and make it perfect." "Perfect, what planet are you from this world is not perfect!" interrupted Zoey. Jared replied, "Ms. Meijer's you are right this world is very far from perfect and the reason for that is because sin has entered the world." In puzzlement Zoey said, "I thought you said, "sin is when we displease God." Joann answered back, "yes that is what sin is. When the first humans were created. God gave them one rule and they disobey that one rule. As soon as that happened the Earth started to fall apart and it has only gotten worse over time." This sounded very superstitious to Zoey so she asked, "How can you be sure this isn't a load of mythological bull crap." Jared said, "my son and I love astronomy and did you know that there is space debris so large that if it hit the Earth no human could survive. Even, the most conservative figures, of the age of the Earth says that it is seven thousand years old, in that long of time the chances of Earth being hit by a large (doomsday causing) space rock are high and if you want to say the Earth is Billions of years old chances of being hit are even higher. The fact that humanity, both those who believe in God and those that do not believe in any kind of deity are still around shows that God exist and cares about the whole world. This God tells me that sin has entered the world. Therefore, I am apt to believe him.

Then Zoey asked, "What does this have to do with a bloody sheep?" Joann explained that before Jesus came to the Earth. People had to regularly kill sheep and other animals to pay for their sins, because the cost of sin was separation from God." Zoey wasn't sure she wanted anything to do with the cruel God the Redding's were talking about. Her friend went on, "well Jesus lived a sinless life, he was the only one who ever has. Then after only thirty-three years of life he was murdered but his death paid the price of the sins of the whole world, past, present, and future. Now anyone who accepts him as LORD can have their sins forgiven. Zoey commented, "That sounds a little too easy." Jared responded, "I don't know how true it is but, we all have heard stories that there are huge sums of money that go unclaimed every year because people do not take the time to fill out their tax refunds. Well, many people die every year that never take the time to accept Jesus. Which is a great shame because Jesus not only wants to keep you out of Hell, he wants to walk with you and be your friend and support you through this difficult world we live in."

As they were talking the waiter arrived with a giant pizza. A pizza so large there was barely any room for them to eat and/or to sit the pitcher of pop down. So, the waiter grabbed an unused table and sat the pizza on this table. They very much enjoyed their lunch. Max was not use to eating out with so much delicious food so he devoured his food like a starving wild animal. Joann worried that since he was eating so fast, he might chock.

As they were eating Joann asked her friend, "do you have any more questions?" Zoey said, "I have more questions. But the first one is, are you just being nice to me because you want something out of me or do you really want to be my friend." Joann replied, "I want to be your friend. It was not that long ago I too was raising a preschooler and

I am aware of the stress you must be under." Scuffing up her husband's hair she said, "I was blessed to have a loving husband who gave me all the support I could ask for yet, there were days I just wanted to scream and pull my hair out. Yes, I would love for you to become a Christian. But, even if you never chose to accept Christ, I still want to be a loyal friend to you and support you as a fellow mother."

That evening at the Redding's home

As the Joann and Jared were getting ready for bed, Joann was flustered from her lunch with Zoey. "Jared what more can I do about Zoey? I love the girl and I know she is not in a good place right now. Ah! I want to help her yet I know my own speech is too filled with churchesse and I don't know have to get past myself!" Said Joann in frustration." Jared responded, "Jo you have got to see it from her point of view. She just walked into a place where everyone knows and speaks fluently a lingo that is not just foreign to her, but the ideas behind the language have never even been comprehended." Joann said, "That does not help." Jared wished he had the answers his wife was looking for but all he could say is, "Sorry Jo but Spiritual matters are God's department not mine. The only and best thing you can do is pray for and love Ms. Meijers. But Joann dear I will be praying for you two women and you know I am always here to support you."

That next afternoon as Zoey came to pick up her son. Joann said, "Ms. Meijers, I very much enjoy having your son in class. He is a great kid and oh what an imagination he has. You must be proud to have Max as a son." Joann replied, "Why are you suddenly flattering me?" Joann said, because I can tell you need it. Have you given any thought to my offer to babysit Max?" Zoey said, "Yes, I have, but I am trying to save your offer for an emergency. I do not want to use your offer futilely. Joann said, "It was not a onetime offer and the fact that you are concerned about abusing my kindness makes me want to help you all the more. As I said, "you need to take some time to yourself to recharge your batteries in order for you to be the mother you want to be even, if it is just to take a nice hot soaking bath without worrying about a three-year-old barging in or getting into some other kind of trouble.

Wednesday

Most days had been hard days for Zoey Meijers since becoming a single mother. Wednesday was an exceptionally hard day. It started out like most days, however, as she left Max's school, she got caught behind farm equipment. Normally there is just enough time for her to get to work from dropping Max off at head-start with her going 55mph almost the whole way but today she was forced to go and the traffic was too heavy to get around the equipment notwithstanding her horn honking and use of profanity the driver would not go. He remained in front of her long enough to make her thirty minutes late for work. When she arrived, her supervisor chewed her out for being late. Later that day her machine decided to act up and cover her in oil. At lunch, she had to call a babysitter to pick Max up from school because she had to work an hour over her normal day.

She was burned out so, she remembered Joann's offer she called Joann and said, "Mrs. Redding if tonight works for you I really need to take you up on your offer to babysit Max." Joann replied, "Ah, sure I can watch him tonight." What Joann did not let on is Wednesday their whole family normally goes to the mid-week service at church but, she did not want Zoey to feel guilty so she said nothing. When she got off the phone she told her husband to take Jarome to church she had to babysit tonight. However, Jared replied, "Honey serving Zoey is more important we all will watch her son."

Max was excited to see Mrs. Redding and Jarome. Jarome played with Max like he was Max's big brother. They played kickball outside and after it started to get dark they came in and played trucks. Joann fixed spaghetti for dinner. After dinner Joann read Max a bedtime story and he fell asleep. It was not long after this Zoey arrived to pick up her son. Zoey thanked the Redding family and said, you have no idea how much I needed tonight and what it meant to me that you watched Max." Joann then said, "we enjoyed having him, I hope we can have him over again sometime."

Next Sunday Morning

Just like the week before Max really wanted to attend Sunday school. The people Zoey had talked to the week before seemed like nice people. Nevertheless, their churchy lingo freaked her out so as Zoey was driving her son to church, she told him.

"Now Max, I'm allowing you to go to church on one condition when Sunday school is over you come out and find me I will be sitting in the car. If you have any problems go talk to Mrs. Redding." Shortly after dropping Max off the Redding family arrived. Joann asked Zoey, "What are you doing out here?" Zoey replied anxiously, "I can't go through another time like last week church is just too weird." Joann replied, "That is cool I can understand that. But just out of curiosity's sake what if there was a Sunday school class that was free of all the things that made that class so bizarre a place where you could ask all your questions as they come up would you go? Zoey answered, "I don't know maybe."

Now reader this chapter cannot do this subject justice. We may wish that your own friends and family would choose to accept the Lord just because we ask them to but most of the time it is not that easy. As Paul said in 1 Corinthians 3:6, "I planted the seed, Apollos watered it, but God has been making it grow. *" Our job is just to love the world as Jesus loved the world and share the good news. If people do not respond when you share the gospel it is not your fault but we must be ready to share our faith when the spirit gives us an open door. However, we in the twenty-first century have a unique problem that many past generations have not had. Not all but, many of the people we encounter do not have any kind of religious background. Therefore, many of our basic christianesse terms will be a foreign language to them. Many do not even know basic concepts like what is sin, Jesus was a historical person or even how the Bible is organized. As a result, the simple truth of the gospel MUST be presented in a simple way.

1. What is your church doing to reach out to the community outside your walls? What are you doing to reach non-believers around you? What more can you do?

2. What can you and your church do, to make it easier for visitor to understand what is going on without watering down the message?

Chapter 9

Steve awoke to great physical pain. It was so great he thought he was going to die. He did not have a close relationship with any of his congregation therefore he called the person who he was the closest to, Carissa, his secretary. He felt awkward about asking a woman to come over to his home when no one else was going to be present but this was an emergency.

He called her up and said, "Carissa I think I'm having a heart attack. I need you to take me to the hospital." She rushed to get ready, knowing that Steve was not a hypochondriac. Carissa brought Steve to the hospital. He was given several tests which revealed that his blood pressure was off the charts. His stress level was so high that the doctors were surprised he didn't have previous problems.

The doctor who examined Steve asked him about his profession. When Steve said, he was a pastor, the doctor said, "That doesn't surprise me. Pastors often have problems with stress. You must tell your congregation that they need to take some of the responsibility off your shoulders."

The idea of doing this scared Pastor Palmer. First, because he was a bit frightened to delegate responsibilities, he feared his people wouldn't step up and do. Second, he liked to know what was going on at all times and to have control over the details. Word reached the leadership of St. Thomas Church about Pastor Palmer's health problems. Many weren't sure what to do. They considered calling Pastor Skull Daniels who was pastor of their daughter church in Cadillac, Michigan. Pastor Daniels had filled in for Pastor Palmer in the past but. The elders, however sensed that they were to do something unthinkable, they were going to wait on the Lord and let God direct the service.

When it was time for the sermon no one knew who would be giving the message. The message that morning was given by God Himself. If you were not a follower of God, it would have seemed weird or, you may not have even noticed. However, for the children of God the Presence of their Father and Lord couldn't have been clearer. It was as if He were standing there face-to-face in the flesh before them. Everyone knew it was God speaking that day.

The service started with an extended time of praise and worship. Numerous people spoke up and told about how God was working in their lives. One man said that the Lord was calling him to give of himself. Others felt they were supposed to do even scarier things. They were called to wait on the Lord and let Him take control of their plans. Edna spoke up and said, "I'm elderly and I don't like leaving my home on these cold, snowy days but I need to be willing to bear the weather and visit those in the nursing home. It is only by the grace of God I ain't there now."

Every time the worship leaders turned around another person was confessing their unwillingness to serve God. They then committed to serve Him with the gifts they were given. That afternoon Pastor Palmer returned home to an answering machine full of messages. They were not the cries for help as he feared they would be. They were cries of "How can I help you?"

Discussion Questions

1. Does God still speak directly to people? If so, what should our response be? (Acts 2:17-21)

2. If you are a leader in your church, are you overworked? If you are, what should you do so that you are not so overwhelmed and can be as effective as possible?

3. Have you obeyed God when He asked you to do something that seemed to not make sense? If so, what has God asked you to do?

4. How can you use your gifts and talents for the Lord's service?

5. How well are you living for Jesus?

Chapter 10

Ten Years Ago

Matthew McFall grew up in a nice home. His father was a salesman who could sell anything to anyone and rarely was turned down. But when he was turned down, he knew how to make that person feel like they had made the biggest mistake of their life, even if the product was useless junk. His mother on the other hand was a nice godly woman who hated her husband's knack for swindling. As a child, Matthew looked up to his mother. He loved how lovely her faith was but the siren song of money was too great. Now reader please don't get me wrong, money in and of itself is neither good nor evil but, the love of it reeks of hell itself. Too bad the poisonous smell of hell often smells irresistible to us humans.

Modern Day

Matthew was a hard-working boy whose work often paid off. He started off doing yardwork for people and those people showed him how to do different household repairs so he added handyman services to his repertoire. Because he was such a skilled and hard worker people kept recommending his services to their friends and family. The only problem he ever seemed to face was the other boys in the neighborhood who kept getting mad at him for stealing away all their business. He would always tell his competition, "Business is business". After sometime he had more business than he could handle so he offered to let the other boys work for him. He gave them business and he took a cut of the money from each job, without having to do any real physical labor.

One day, one of the boys who work for him went on vacation with his family so he could not do his jobs for that week. Therefore, Matthew covered for him. While he was doing yardwork at Mrs. Van Amsterdam's house he discovered she was having an Ever-Brown party. Mrs. Van Amsterdam sold Ever-Brown cookware to the other senior citizens who lived around her, to supplement her late husband's pension and Social Security.

When he finished with her work, she invited him in for a pop and to cool off. He acted like he wanted to move on knowing that being direct about his curiosity, about what those ladies were talking about could make him look pushy or worse. But, when Mrs. Van Amsterdam insisted, he stay, he asked, "what are you ladies doing?" One of the lady said, "oh nothing to concern yourself with young man. We are having and Ever-Brown party. Ever-Brown is a line of cookware that is often bought and sold by older women like us." Matthew thought to himself, "really? I bet with the contacts I've made through my handy man/lawn care business I can have these women working for me in no time at all." Matthew said, "is there a minimum age for selling Ever-Brown?" These ladies said, "no however you're just a teenager. It just is not done this way." Yet, they decided "let's just humor him. Who knows, he might just be able to sell the stuff."

To their surprise not only was Matthew able to sell Ever-Brown merchandise, he had the best first week sales for that area ever! His success in selling products resulted in him moving up in the company. He overshot the progress of other people so before long he became a distributor. Making money was like a God for Matthew. He would do and say anything if it meant another sale. However, if others got hurt along the way Matthew didn't care.

There was a girl named Ann, she was a nice sweet friendly girl. She was rather plain in the eyes of man but, her heart made her a knockout. She was a true daughter of king Jesus. There was not anyone who didn't know she was a Christian. She tried to witness to everyone she knew but, she didn't force her faith on anyone.

Matthew, who was attending the same high school as Ann said to himself, "hmm, if this plain Jane was able to "sell" her religion that easily. I wonder what she can do with something of real value. So, he started putting his bad boy charm on her. He reeled in many other girls but Ann seemed immune to all his best moves. He asked around to find out "What's wrong with this chick? I tried everything to get her attention and she just ignores me. What is going on with her?" The people he talked to said, " She is a Christian and she won't date anyone who isn't a Christian too. Then he asked, 'do you know where she goes to church?' The people he talked to said how should we know, we aren't religious nuts. Matthew was determined to get that girl on his side so he kept asking around until he learns her place of worship.

Eventually Matthew found out where she attended church. Fulfilling his devious plan wasn't as easy as he hoped it would be. Matthew was counting on Ann to be a desperate girl who would just jump at the chance to date a guy like him, but to his surprise Ann was more annoyed than flattered to see him. Matthew had grown up going to church therefore he knew the lingo but, he hadn't stepped through the doors of a church building since his mother died four years earlier. When he saw Ann he went over and shook her hand and said, "Oh, it's so nice to see you here Miss Ann. I didn't know you attended this fellowship." He knew this would look odd but he knew he had to get her attention.

As any good Christian girl, she was civil to him on the outside but on the inside, she was thinking, "Get away from me you creep, I want nothing to do with you. I can see right through your act." However, coming to this church wasn't a total loss. He knew he had to be patient and let these people get to know him. But he discovered that some of the people here particularly the older people were willing to buy and sell from each other.

He said nothing about Ever-Brown nevertheless, when the timing was right and he sensed that people considered him one of their own he sprain the trap and he started selling. At first, some of the other people thought that it was nice to see a young person trying to earn a little extra money. Yet, before anyone knew it, Matthew had tricked almost everyone into buying cookware and Matthew took off with their money never to be seen again.

Discussion Questions

1. Is money good or evil? Why or why not? (1 Timothy 6:10, Hebrews 13:5)

2. Why does it seem like people can't fail while others are unable to succeed? (Ecclesiastes 6, Psalms 12:5, Isaiah 49:24-26)

3. How do you spot a con-artist like Matthew? How do you avoid getting sucked in by one? (Matthew 7:15, Leviticus 19:19, John 10, Acts 9, Acts 8:9-25)

4. How do you judge what "real value" is? (Philippians 4:8, Matthew 7:1-6, Ephesians 1, Matthew 6:19-20

Chapter 11

Cash was a smart young high schooler. He was popular. He had everything going for him but, it was all about to change for him the day he graduated from high school. Cash's parents didn't have a lot of money to send him to college. Thus, they felt that he should take a year off before going to college so he can earn some money to pay for college the next year.

Since most of the people around his age had gone off to college his social life was rather lonely. In high school, he had an active social life. Now he was having trouble finding anyone whose schedule fit his own enough to find time to get a cup of coffee.

As a teenager, he was always active in church, so he was looking forward to the first Sunday as a young adult however, he was in for a cruel surprise. When he got to Sunday school he discovered for the first time in his life there was no Sunday school class for him. Some wanted him to continue with the youth group. Cash may have been rather immature yet, he was no longer a high schooler so he didn't fit in. As for adult Sunday school classes the class that fit him best was filled with young married people. Thus, he felt very uncomfortable. No one openly condemned cash for his singleness in fact everyone kept saying, "oh you are blessed to be a young single man. "Yet, in a room full of married people it is easy to feel like a weirdo and begin to question, "how can you serve God with your singleness in this world that seems obsessed with paring off?"

Cash wasn't sure what to do so, he decided to talk to his pastor about his concerns. His pastor said, "no, there is nothing wrong with being single. In fact, the apostle Paul said "Now for the matter you wrote about; it is good for a man not to marry. I would like you to be free from concern. And unmarried man is concerned about the Lord's affairs. How he can please the Lord. But a married man is concerned about the affairs of this world and how he can please his wife and his interests are divided." It wasn't that Paul was against marriage, he just felt that if you were blessed enough to be single and could handle it, then it is better to remain single.

Pastor Palmer then said, "I know how it feels to be single in a world that seems to act as if there is something wrong with being unattached. I dated girls in college but never found the one I sensed God wanted me to marry. Marriage is one of the most special commitments that a person can make and should not be entered lightly. Not everyone is called to marry, however you can pray even now that the Lord helps you to know and to be obedient to his will." So, that is just what Cash did, he prayed to the Lord for wisdom and discernment to know who the Lord has chosen to be his wife. In the meantime, cash asked the Lord to help him to accept and to use his singleness wisely and to the glory of God.

Discussion Questions

1. Is there anything wrong with being single? If not, how do we support single people? If you are single how do you use your gift of being single to the fullest of the glory of God? (1 Corinthians 7:1)

2. Is there anything wrong with marriage? If not, how do you know if you should get married?

3. How do we help people who truly are trying to seek God, but whose needs are not being met in our fellowship?

4. What is our church doing to reach out to young adults?

Chapter 12

The question of how to serve God when you are single in a world that is obsessed with pairing off, was only to be the first drop in an ocean of questions that would seek to drown Cash. The next year when he started college, he met many kinds of people with a myriad of beliefs. All these ideas caused his head to spin. To try and get some grounding in his life, Cash found a Christian college group. This group only added to Cash's confusion, for in this group there were people who shared his faith. However, Cash never knew how different their expressions of faith could be from his own.

In this group, there were Catholics, Calvinists, Pentecostals, and even Seventh-Day Adventists. Cash always prided himself on his non-denominational views. But now he started to wonder what the truth is. Was the tradition he grew up in wrong? If not, can we all be right?

Thus, Cash did what we all should do. He searched the scriptures to find the truth. All throughout the Bible, it talks about men and women of God doing amazing things through the power of the Holy Spirit. At first, this sounded weird but, it wasn't like cash could fight with God. Then he started to see a new aspect of the Holy Spirit in Matthew 3:16c. "The spirit of god descended like a dove and settling on him" ** and in acts 16:6b it says, "The holy spirit had prevented them from preaching the word in the province of Asia at the time." ** He had read these stories countless times yet Cash had always thought of the Holy Spirit as some abstract force. Now he agreed the spirit was a personal member of the god head He is and this was what He able to learn from the Pentecostals.

The tradition he grew up in acknowledged that the spirit existed and was an equal member of the God-head nevertheless they only talked about the Holy Spirit casually.

In Catholicism, there were many things that he didn't find any support for. Yet, he found they were not without base for their beliefs. Peter was called the 'rock' on which the church would be built. The biggest thing Cash received from Catholicism and other liturgical traditions was a reverence for the things of God which, too often, he treated so flippantly.

There were other revelations Cash made that he so wished weren't true. Yet, he couldn't argue with the word of God such as, predestination ran truly opposite to the way he was taught. Cash asked his pastor about the Calvinist doctrines of predestination and election. "Pastor, I have read in Romans that God chooses who will be saved and who won't. This must be a mistake." Pastor Palmer said, "I'm sorry to say that it's no mistake. I too do not understand how predestination and election can be balanced with free will. Yet, scripture clearly says The Lord isn't really being slow about his promises, as some people think. No, he is being patient for your sake. He does not want anyone to be destroyed, but wants everyone to repent." (2 Peter 3:9)** We, are not God. Nor, should we think that we are anything close to His level. We need to trust that he loves us and that He will work it all out. Cash didn't like this answer but he had to admit his pastor was right. This wasn't the only thing that boggled his mind about what he discovered from this Scripture.

He also wondered why Christians worshipped God on a Sunday when, since the beginning of time, the Sabbath was on Saturday. Pastor Palmer's answer wasn't very satisfying to Cash. Pastor Palmer said, "The early church celebrated the Lord's Day on Sunday because that was the day Jesus rose from the dead." This seemed like a weak answer to Cash, so he continued to wonder about that issue. For each of us, some issues are easier to accept than others. Cash had no problem accepting the idea of being led by the spirit and giving the Holy Spirit his due respect. He also had no problem with showing God reverence. Yet, other issues were harder to swallow.

Cash knew that if predestination is true, his unbelieving friends and relatives might never have a chance to know God. At the same time, he had to balance it with other scriptures. "No don't say that. Who are you, a mere human being, to argue with God? Should the thing that was created to say to the one who created it, 'why have you made me like this?' When a potter makes jars out of clay to make one for decoration and another to throw garbage into? In the same way, even though God has the right to show his anger and his power, he is very patient with those on whom his anger falls. Who are therefore destined for destruction?" * This passage points out that God is in control and it is not right for us to question God. We humans would be foolish to think we know who will be saved and who won't. Cash and we as well need to let God be God. However, as it says in 2 Peter 3:9, "the Lord is not slow in keeping his promises, as some understand slowness. He is patient with you, not wanting anyone to perish, but everyone to come to repentance." * This means that God doesn't want anyone to turn their backs to him and just when you may think your loved one is beyond hope and spiritually lost forever, God can yet open their eyes.

1. How do we make sense of all the belief systems there are in the world?

2. How do we young people deal with all the ideas that we encounter as we go through young adulthood?

3. What things could your local church learn from other churches?

Chapter 13

The 1920s

Many years ago, long before Pastor Steven Palmer ever breathed a single breath there was a church called New New Deli Wesleyan Methodist Church in New New Deli, Michigan. It was a typical church and it was the center of the New New Delian culture. Both city and country folks alike flocked to this church on Sunday.

People who lived even as far away as Hartlin traveled the fifteen-mile journey to New New Deli to hear the word of God. Today, fifteen miles might not seem like that long of a distance but in the day when few, if anyone owned a car. It was quite a sacrifice to hitch up the horses to travel to church. Eventually, some of the farming families started to complain. Howard Jasup who was one of the most vocal of the families from Hartlin went to talk to the council of New New Deli Wesleyan Methodist church. "The fifteen-mile journey from Hartlin to New New Deli is too much of a strain on our families. We want to be involved in what goes on here yet, how can we when New New Deli is so far away? We are demanding that this church plant another in Hartlin. We the church members from Hartlin believe in this so strongly we are willing to give up portions of our own land for the construction of this church."

The council thought this was a nice start however, their biggest concern wasn't addressed. "Where will they get, the resources needed to start a church?" When asked that question Howard said, "In the 1800's it wasn't uncommon for preachers to ride a circuit. Is it too much to ask Pastor Kelly to do the same thing?" (Hiram Kelly was 76 years old and for many people he was the only preacher they could remember leading them.) The council said, "I'm sorry but that is just too much to ask of Pastor Kelly, he is just too old to be doing all that rough traveling every week!" Their answer didn't please Howard one bit. It took every ounce of will power he had to not talk back and say, "Yes, but you are asking people much older to make that trip every week!"

The church members from Hartlin met together and decided that they wanted the support from New New Deli Wesleyan Methodist Church. However, if they are not going to give it then too bad. Starting a church in Hartlin was too important, they would start one with or without the support of the church in New New Deli.

The church first started as tent meetings then it was held where the Newcome farm, Jasup and the Smith farms all met together. Some thought Howard Jasup should do the preaching but it was decided that he was too hot tempered to lead a church. So, instead they chose Tommy Merrimaker who was the youngest son of a business man who was trying to open a factory in this farming community. They named the church St. Thomas Church after the apostle who insisted on seeing the resurrected Christ himself. He then went on to bring the gospel to India. The founders of St. Thomas Church said, "We want to hunger for the truth like Thomas."

St. Thomas Church had wonderful ideals yet, from the time of its birth in had a secret disease that it would not admit even to itself. The viruses of unforgiveness and hate. They hated New New Deli Wesleyan Methodist Church for not supporting them when they just wanted to start a church in their own community. As all viruses do it kept growing for nearly a century until these issues were dealt. It caused division between these two church that should be as close as family, to have as little to do with one another as oil and water.

Discussion Questions

1. What are your feelings about church planting? Is church planting Biblical or just a fad? (Mathew. 28:16-20, Acts 1:6-8, Acts 2:14-77)

2. Are you willing to stand up and sacrifice for what you believe God is calling you to do?

3. Is it right to start a church out of anger?

4. Are you hungry for the truth?

Chapter 14

Ten Years Ago

With a vroom and a cur-dunk Steve Palmer pulled into the driveway of his new home. It was a nice three-bedroom parsonage, too big for Steven to know what to do with. While he was unpacking, a hairy tattoo covered man with hair that was so long that it came below his shoulders, came outside to mow his lawn. Steve was excited to meet his neighbors so he walked over and introduced himself to him. Some of his church members who were helping him move in however, didn't think it was as good of an idea as Steve did but, he didn't care. He walked over and held out his hand and said, "Hello, I'm Steve and you are?" The neighbor said, "I'm Skull." Then Steve noticed Skull's motorcycle and said, "Cool hog, I used to ride when I was in college. It was nowhere near as nice, mind you but, it got me where I needed to go." After a moment of silence Steve said, "I better get back to moving in."

That coming Monday Steve went to the Secretary of State's office to get his Pennsylvania driver's license transferred to Michigan. To his surprise there was Skull; all dressed up in casual dress clothes and a name tag that said "Dwayne." Skull said, "Oh, you are from Pennsylvania. What brought you to Michigan?" Steve said, "Work." Dwayne said, "Really?" Yet inside he was thinking, "how dare a fucking bastard" like you take away a good job from the citizens of Michigan who probably have been looking for quite some time for work." Steve wasn't sure what was bothering Skull but he could tell by the look on Dwayne's face that he did something to upset him, so he left as quickly as he could yet, Steve knew that it was no accident that he ran into Skull again. Before he started his car to go home, he said a quick prayer for Skull. "LORD, I don't know what is going on or what you are planning to do. But LORD Jesus whatever your plan is, just use me and keep me from messing your plans up amen."

Later that same day Steve was coming home from the store (to pick up some things to make dinner with that night.) When he noticed in front of him a semi-truck getting too close to a motorcyclist, then suddenly the motorcycle was pushed off the road. Only by the grace of God did the rider get off his bike in time. The motorcycle rolled down a hill and was crushed by a truck going down the free-way below. Steve stopped to help the rider and when he did he discovered it was skull. Skull wasn't too happy to see Steve yet, he wasn't going to complain. His bike was totaled and he needed a ride home.

On the ride home Skull asked Steve why he had stopped to help him on such a busy road. Steve said, "Because you needed help." He was glad for the help but he was thinking, "That is kind of a dumb answer, only an idiot would stop and help a stranger on the side of the road. I could have been a car jacker for all he knew. I certainly wouldn't have helped somebody along the road. So, Skull asked, "What's your deal? You a pastor or something or are you just plain stupid? Nobody in their right mind would pull over to help someone on the side of a highway overpass, not to mention someone that looks like a roughneck like me. I could have been planning to steal your car for all you knew." Steve said, "Well you are right and probably many people have the fears you expressed, that is probably why there is a Good Samaritan Law. However, you needed help what else was I supposed to do?" Skull then asked, "So you are a doctor?" Steve said, "No, but I train people how to deliver lifesaving information. That left Skull confused so he said, "What the hell does that mean? You a pastor, an EMT or do you do something else? "I am a pastor.", said Steve. Skull wasn't too hot on anything having to do with religion nevertheless, the more Steve and Skull got to know each other the more they got along.

While Skull waited to get his check from his insurance company, Steve volunteered to drive him wherever he needed to go. When his insurance check came Steve drove Skull to the motorcycle dealership in New New Deli. On the way, there Skull said, "How'd a bastard like you end up becoming a pastor? Excuse my language." Steve said, "Well I grew up going to church. I assumed I was a Christian until I was in High School. I was playing on the basketball team. The captain of our team was a very tall guy named Jackson Flowers, he was a basketball machine. At 6'10" he was built for doing nothing else but shooting baskets. Well, we were playing in the regional game, if we won it we were going to the state championship game.

We were down to the last few seconds of the game and in the excitement, Jackson fouled a member of the opposing team. The ref didn't have to call a foul, Jackson told on himself. As you can imagine Jackson wasn't too popular after that. I asked him later why he didn't let it go and he said, "I wasn't going to win that way. If I won, I wanted to win the way Jesus would win." I thought that was rather a dweeby answer but it got me thinking about my own Christian life. Am I really a Christian or do I just claim to be? I want to stand up for something real. From that point on I decided I was going to stand up for something real and teach others to do the same. Then Skull said, "Where do you preach?" Steve replied, "St. Thomas Church." When they got to the motorcycle shop, they saw many wonderful bikes. Skull picked out such a beautiful bike that it made Steve jealous that he could never afford anything so nice but, this hog was twice the price of Skull's insurance check.

As they parted ways Skull said, "I will be checking your church out. I don't have to dress up, do I?" Steve said, "No the way you are dressed now is fine." Skull was dressed like any stereotypical biker. He was expecting that his friend Steve was going to say, "Yes please do." 68 But, when Steve said that his biker garb was fine, he was stuck he had to go check out his friend's church.

When Skull pulled into the driveway of the little country church, everybody could hear the roar of his motorcycle. Daringly Skull parked, he was convinced that entering the doors of St. Thomas Church was a bad idea but, if he didn't his friend could say, "You didn't even check my church out." With a deep breath, he walked in the door. The warm greeting, he received surprised him.

Everyone was quick to shake his hand and show him around. He was treated like a honored guest. He wanted to say, "These people don't trust me" however, he was greeted with open arms. As a result, he was forced to abandon this idea.

When it was time for the worship service, people showed him the way to the sanctuary yet, the biggest help was the sound of the organ music. Finally, he found something to complain about, this music was so dull he knew he was sure to fall asleep. It wasn't anything like the rock music they played in the bars, where he spent most of his free time. After more "hims" as they called them, at least that's what he thought they called the songs they sang. Then, they collected money. The only reason he didn't leave right away was his friend Pastor Steve Palmer said, "If you are new here (which Skull was) please don't give." So, he was given permission to keep his hard-earned cash.

After, the offering was taken up. Some old dude Skull didn't know started praying out loud. He was thinking about taking off but he decided that probably wasn't such a good idea since he told his friend he was coming, so he thought he better be on the bench to be seen. However, this old guy kept droning on and on before Skull knew it, he was asleep.

When Skull woke up Steve was already behind the podium. "For he has set a day when he will judge. He has given proof of this to all men by raising him from the dead." Acts 17:31 *Steve read aloud. Now some of you may be saying that's for the other guy sitting next to me, I'm a good person. I've got nothing to worry about. If you think this you might want to look at Romans 3:23 where it says, "For all have sinned and fallen short of the glory of God." * Now you may say, "That is fine however, I don't believe in a God. There is no proof he is real." All I can say about that is, Oh really? As the Apostle Paul pointed out in Romans 1:20, "For since the creation of the world God's invisible qualities, his eternal power and divine nature have been clearly seen being understood from what has been made, so that men are without excuse." * You may say but science has proven that random chance created the world. I say that is like dropping a box of car parts from a skyscraper and expecting a car to magically come together. No wait, the creation of the universe is even harder than that, because the universe had to have a beginning for evolution to be true, there had to be chemicals to start with. Where did the chemicals come from? Answer, God created the universe out of nothing. Therefore, there must be a God we must answer to. Yet, before you feel too depressed let me tell you, there is a solution to our sin problem. In Romans 10:9 it says If you confess with your mouth, "Jesus is Lord." If you believe with your heart that God raised him from the dead, you will be saved." * It is supposed to be that simple you ask? It's a gift so to receive it, you need to be humble enough to ask for it. You will never be good enough to be saved by your own good deeds.

This sermon gave Skull a lot to think about. Before Skull went home, he asked his friend, "Do you really believe the BS that you spouted today?" Steve answered. "Yes."

The words of Steve kept nagging at Skull, which caused him to remember his Grandmother. He hadn't talked to her in some time. Thus, he picked up the phone and called her. When the phone was picked-up it was his grandmother's in-home care taker. She said, "Your grandma can't talk now she is on her way to the hospital! Before he could get the details, the phone clicked off. So after making sure she was at the county general hospital he raced over to see her.

"Is that you Dwayne?" said Skull's grandmother. Skull replied "Yes Grandma. I don't know why I didn't come sooner." His grandmother said, "That's ok, what matters is, you are here now. Dwayne, I'm on my way home, I am sure of it. I just want you to know I'm excited to go home to the Father" This statement wasn't much comfort to Skull because he was convinced that there is no afterlife, and he wasn't sure what she was talking about. Before, he could say anything else, "… Beeeeep!" She was gone.

The next day Steve and Skull met for a cup of coffee before going to work. Skull asked Steve, "Your job has something to do with the afterlife, right?" "I guess you could say that" replied Steve. Then Skull asked, "Then answer me this, how can anyone be so sure there is an afterlife?" Steve thought for a moment and then said, "Well I know there is a God and he tells me there is a Heaven and a Hell. I believe my God doesn't lie so; they must exist." Skull at this point got to the point of this discussion, "My grandmother died yesterday. She sounded excited to be dying? This makes no sense; how can anyone be excited to die?" Steve asked, "Did she know the LORD Jesus as her savior?" Skull said, "I guess she did, she certainly talked about him enough." Steve replied, "Well then, I have your answer if she was a Christian then she is now with Jesus who is the lover of her soul. She was excited because she is now in a place where all her worries are gone."

"Well good for her! But I don't believe in such fairy tales," replied Skull. Steve then asked, "What if you are wrong? Is eternity in Hell worth betting with? If I'm wrong I might not please all my carnal wants as much as I might want to. If you are wrong, you will be in a never-ending nightmare."

Skull was silenced. He realized his friend made a good point however, he liked his life and if he acted like most of the Christians, he knew that would be an act for him, something he was opposed to doing. Sensing his friend's concerns, he said, "Being a Christian is not about fitting into any other mold than the mold of Christ who was all about loving God with all of his soul, heart, strength and mind, and loving his fellow human beings as he loved himself. Christianity is not about a religion. It's about a relationship, having a friend who will be there when and where no one else can be. So, is there anything here that is contradictory to being a biker? Skull wanted to say, "Yes." For this sounded too good to be true but if that is all there is to it, it sounded good to him. So, he said, "If there is no catch, sign me up, I'm in." Steve said, "In Romans 10:9 it says that if you confess with your mouth, "Jesus is LORD, believe in your heart that God raised him from the dead, you will be saved; * so do you?" Skull said, "Sure I guess." He wasn't sure about this Christianity thing but he was willing to check it out. So, Steve said, "If you want to be a follower of Christ, say this prayer with me. "LORD Jesus, I know I've done many things I shouldn't have yet; the Bible says if I ask I will be forgiven. I ask for your forgiveness. I want to be yours from now on. Amen."

Skull's faith and knowledge of Christ kept growing. He became a mighty warrior for God. It wasn't long before St. Thomas Church looked more like a motorcycle rally than a small country church each Sunday. Steve loved his friend as a brother in the LORD. Nevertheless, after sometime of seeing increasingly number of these new believers who were different from their 72 core members, the elders started to ask themselves if this was God's way of saying it is time to plant a new church. Some said, "We don't want these baby Christians to feel unwelcome, besides they breathe new life into our church that was getting too stuffy. Others said, "We are not trying to kick them out. Anyone who wishes to stay is welcome to yet, we can't be selfish we must free them to reach people who we would struggle to reach. So, it was decided that Skull would be mentored and groomed to be the pastor of a biker church. He would be made an associate pastor given a chance to preach once a month and wherever, Pastor Palmer needed a fill-in. For the next five years as plans were worked out, Skull was trained to be a pastor. During the last six months before going on their own, the core team members of Journey's End Biker Church met in the basement of St. Thomas Church during the main service for practice services.

On the last Saturday night of October they met for their first service on their own. They leased an old bar that had gone out of business in Cadillac. When they started St. Thomas Church couldn't be prouder.

Discussion Questions

1. If you see someone in need what should you do?

2. Are you willing to lose in your personal life to win in your Christian walk? (1 Corinthians 4:1-5, James 1:22-25, 27, James 2:18-20, 24)

3. How should we treat new people in our church who we are personally uncomfortable with? (Acts 10)

4. What should be our motivation for church planting? (Matthew 28:16-20)

Chapter 15

Eight Years Ago

The birth of Journey's End Biker Church was an easy birth. At least, from the outside it appeared easy, so easy some would ask, "Why wasn't it started sooner." Others have asked was a new church needed?

When Skull Daniels first visited St. Thomas Church, he was an odd ball. The congregation tried to show him Christ like love but Skull felt out of place. Skull was a crude foul mouth, tattooed covered leather-bound motorcycle riding brut. Whereas St. Thomas Church was a stuck-up stereotypical church stuck in the traditions of the past. However, God was about to use this mismatch to help both become what God would have them become. When Pastor Palmer first invited Skull to his church, Skull found the hymns and organ music to be too old fashion. The Sunday School was nice yet, aimed more at farmers than a white-collar clerk like himself. Skull would have left without giving St. Thomas Church a fair chance if it hadn't been for the fact that he promised his friend Steve that, he would be there. After, he accepted the LORD as his Savior he became a regular attender. Nevertheless, Skull didn't change overnight.

Skull was still Skull so even though he knew better, foul words still flowed out of his mouth. He drank less but he still enjoyed a beer now and then with his buddies. However, he was never much of a drinker to begin with. So, what changed you may ask? What changed is that he knew the LORD and he wanted to tell everyone about Him.

Some of his co-workers would say to him, "Well it's about time you grew-up and got religion." Others didn't believe a roughneck like him could ever find God, if he did it wouldn't last. His biker friends laughed at him and razzed him by saying things like, "What's a asshole 75 like you doing in church. You ain't getting soft on us, are you motherfucker, are you?" Skull relied, "I ain't getting soft and Jesus isn't soft either. It takes a real motherfucker to die for a bunch of ass holes like us. God says that if we don't accept his gift of salvation we are screwed, heading to Hell.

His friend Lone wolf complained, "Some God, do it my way or die, no thanks." Skull replied, hey stupid His rules are for our own good. You wouldn't play chicken with a semi would you (unless you are trying to kill yourself.) Well, God is bigger than a semi and he loves us. He isn't trying to take away our fun in fact God says, I have come that you may have life and life more fully. So, Skull challenged his friends, he said, "If you are so tough I dare you to meet me at St. Thomas Church and to sit through the entire service."

Most of Skull's friends showed up that Sunday. When the bikes started pulling into the parking lot it broke the normally calm environment. They knew Skull had been attending yet, a herd of roughnecks caused some people to become rather nervous. They walked in with all the external confidence that you would expect them to have but, inside they were more intimidated by these church people than, the bikers bothered the church people. Lone Wolf, Mad dog (Skull's girlfriend), Hell Raiser and his old lady Viper were convinced that these stuck-up church people would reject them. They were not surprised that some people were a bit nervous around them. Yet, most of the people greeted them warmly.

After service an older man stopped them as they were trying to quietly and quickly depart. He introduced himself and said, "It was nice to see some new faces in our fellowship." They were surprised by a comment, made by a middle-aged man so they responded by saying, "Oh ok, whatever." Then the man continued by saying, "I am Bill this is my wife of twenty-six 76 years of marriage, Clare." He told Hell-raiser, I like your eagle tattoo you have on your face, it looks amazing. Who did the artwork?" Hell-raiser was surprised by the question, "What does this guy know about tats", thought Hell-raiser. So, he replied, "Jo at the Marksman in Traverse City. She is the best tattoo artist in the area." Bill said, "Oh I've heard of her. She is an amazing artist. However, when I got my tats I couldn't afford her high prices so I got mine done locally." Hell-raiser couldn't believe this churchy old guy had tats so he said, "What? You got tattoos?" Bill said, "Oh yes I sure do." I have the names of the four most important ladies in my life." Then he showed them the baby footprint tattoos with the names of his three daughters and then said, "The fourth is a heart shaped tattoo with the name of my wife over my heart. Then his wife blushed. Viper then asked her husband, "Why don't you ever do anything romantic like that for me?"

After Skull's friends' experience at his church, they didn't feel so out of place. They discovered church people weren't much different than they were. When Skull asked his friends what they thought of the service they said, "we felt a little out of place with everyone dressed up. Also, why should we pay to sleep?" Skull replied, "huh?" They said, "the music lulled us to sleep, but the preacher said some profound things.

Skull didn't have much to say about that for that was how he felt when he first came to St. Thomas Church. He talked to his friend Steve about this and Steve said, "Why don't you do a small group Bible study with them. There certainly is praise and worship music that should be more their tempo. Steve helped Skull with the details including how to talk to them about this group meeting. The group grew and grew to the point that other groups were formed out of Skull's group.

As more bikers started attending the worship service leaders started adding more modern worship songs. Some of the older people had to deal with seeing some rather rough looking people at church every week. It was good because it challenged people's ideas of who their neighbors were but it was a rough road that needed to be traveled down for this church.

The elders of St. Thomas Church said it was important for their church to be challenged. However, they recognized that the LORD was telling them it was time to plant a church, a biker church. So, they informed the leadership board of what they were sensing. Many were excited about birthing a new church. Nevertheless, Edna couldn't help but ask, "why should we plant a church? Aren't there already too many churches. We hear about churches closing every day, wouldn't one more church just make the problem worse. Michael Mitchell said, "Mrs. Clyne I understand your objections and they are valid however, what the church elder board is proposing is a church unlike anything around here, a biker church. Brother Skull has started a small group and it has already divided three times and over half those people are coming from as far away as Cadillac. A biker church is needed and Cadillac maybe just the place for it. Consequently, They, therefore agreed to plant this church in Cadillac. Also, they agreed to ask Skull to be its lay pastor.

Steve being the pastor and Skull's friend agreed to approach Skull about pastoring this church plant. Skull liked the idea of there being a church whose ministry was aimed at people like himself. At the same time, he didn't feel qualified to be a pastor, for he was just a common working stiff.

Steve addressed Skull's concerns by saying, "Skull remember the apostles were common people like us. Jesus even chose a government employee like yourself as an apostle. According 78 to, Luke 5:27-32 (Levi who we know as Matthew) was a tax collector." Pastor Palmer then said, "As you know the apostles were the twelve men chosen by our LORD to continue his ministry after his ascension. They were just normal people with normal jobs like: fishermen, a zealot, and a tax collector. Despite their common status, after Jesus left the apostles went all over the world preaching the word of God. Besides I will help you and train you to be a pastor. There is a lot that needs to be done before your church is ready to launch. With this Skull nervously accepted the job.

Skull met with Steve regularly. Skull's knowledge of God's word grew as well as his excitement of planting this church. Yet, it was all positive excitement; as the time drew nearer to the start of this church, the anxiety level also increased in all involved.

The leadership board tried to keep information about this plant church under their hat but, news like this is hard to keep secret for long. The older people had good reason to be worried. For the younger people who had felt stifled by the older people's piano/organ music felt like freedom awaited them in the form of this new church. Therefore, the older people feared the new church could be the death of the church they had built with their own blood, sweat and tears. One evening during a board meeting Bill (who often was the voice of reason said, "Nearly a hundred years ago, your grandparents and great-grandparents were the ones talking of planting this church and they were call rebels and worse. What right do we have, to take away somebody else's right to worship in the style that fits them best. However, I call on you, younger people to stay and grow this church. Help transform St. Thomas Church into the jewel and heart of Hartlin we all know it can be. If you don't, St. Thomas Church's days are numbered. Some of you are called to go and be church planters, others are called to stay. Therefore, all of us should pray for wisdom and discernment."

Because of Bill's words, they spent the rest of the meeting in prayer and listening for God's direction. It was decided that the worship leader would work with the people who would form the praise band. This band would have a twofold purpose first they would develop their talent and become the biker church's band while at the same time training their replacements so that St. Thomas Church could better minister to the next generation.

When it came time for choosing a name, many names were tossed around. Some of the names they considered were: His Place Biker Church, Lord of the Ride Biker Church but, none of those names sounded quite right. Then Viper suggested, Journey's End Biker Church. At first Skull pointed out, "Salvation is not the end of the Journey but, the beginning." To this she replied, "However, the moment you accept Jesus as leader of the pack in your life, is the end of your aimless journey. Christ is now your friend and pack leader who leads us to the better road. After Viper explained this, Journey's End Biker Church is the name they chose.

Some were eager to start services yet, those in leadership knew it was foolish to move too fast. Skull was made an associate pastor while training under Pastor Steve Palmer. Once a month Skull preached the Sunday morning message for the next five years. When it got down to three months before going independent. The start-up team met for practice services, in the basement of St. Thomas Church.

One Year Ago

As for the location, the startup team found a former biker bar that had closed several years ago, The team bought this property and fixed it up yet, kept a lot of the features that were associated with it being a bar. They did this so that the people they are trying to reach would be more comfortable. 80 This wasn't a large space however; it was prefect for the outreach they were trying to do. That first Saturday (for they had their services on Saturday nights.) They had a packed house. Journey End Biker Church was a success.

Discussion Questions

1. Why or why not, should new churches be started? (Acts 1:8, Matthew 28:19-20, John 4:1-42)

2. How should we show Christ like love to people unlike ourselves? (1 Corinthians 9:22)

3. What is the difference between a sin and a taboo? (Exodus 20:1-17)

4. Why are certain things taboos such as: tattoos, body piercing, smoking and drinking (including moderate drinking?) Why do we look down on people who do these things? (1 Corinthians 8:1-13)

5. What are the qualification pastors must meet and what are his/her responsibilities? (Titus 1:6, 1 Timothy 3:2, 1 Timothy 4:6-16, Ephesians 4:11-13

Chapter 16

That Next Winter

He wore shabby clothes and reeked of urine. The skin and hair of this invisible man was dirty and unkempt. Rich (this man's given name.) was as far in economic and social status from his name as any man could get. Most people called him a bum.

Twenty Years Ago

Richard Andrew Smith grew up in as normal of a family as you can get. But, Rich was not normal. Early on his parents could see there was something different about their boy, he had schizophrenia. At times, the medicine worked but the "SP" (as his parents called it) came back with a vengeance.

It would all start with a chill in the air then he would see "Him." He was a dark shadowy figure. Rich would never see his face but Rich knew it was just a matter of time before "Him" would come for him. Sometimes he would be fortunate enough to see the "Woman in the white dress." This person was the opposite of "Him." She was tall and whiter than white. She was so bright that Rich had trouble looking her in the face. As a child, Rich thought she was an angel yet, she had more in common with the demonic than the angelic. Whenever she would appear she would beckon Rich to come to her and he so wanted to. She looked like a savior from his terrifying world. One time, "The woman in the white" dress beckoned him to come to her and he followed her right out a second-floor window. Rich Fell and broke his left arm. His parents thank God that he spared their son's life. However, because of this incident Rich's room was moved to his father's office.

Rich's father had hoped keeping him medicated and away from other people was going to keep him safe, and it did, for a while. Around age twelve the symptoms even appeared to be getting less and less to the point where Rich's parents thought they had seen the last of "Him" and "The Lady in the white dress." One night unexpectedly "Him" came back for revenge! Frantically Rich's parents called every psych ward (they had a number for) in the state of Michigan and the nearest hospital with an open bed wasn't even in Michigan but in Chicago, Illinois. So, they quickly packed up his stuff and headed for Chicago. Rich's parents tried to be brave and positive for their son yet, they themselves truly felt helpless and overwhelmed by fears.

"Will we be attacked on the way to the hospital by our own son? Is there even going to be a place for Rich by the time we reach Chicago?" They could check Rich into the hospital but because of overcrowding the hospital was only able to keep Rich in the psych ward for a short time, (Just long enough to get Rich stabilized.) Thus, it wasn't long before Rich was back in a different psych ward. Going in and out of psych wards became a regular thing for Rich. After high school Rich tried to go to college but his schizophrenia kept him from being able to function so he dropped out. He got lost in his own world even more than before because he ran out of drugs to keep his SP at bay. So, he couldn't keep a job.

Ten Years Ago

Like any other reasonable healthy young man, he loved his parents but, he longed to set out on his own. Tensions grew between his parents and him. So, Rich began the process of signing up for Disability. You would think that with such extraordinary schizophrenia, that hindered his life so severely that it should be easy for him to receive financial help but it was not effortless for him to obtain the help he disparately needed. His doctor had no problem filling out 84 the paperwork he needed to receive disability and yet, his insurance still had to fight to get him his disability money. After a while he obtained his money. At this time, Rich moved in with some friends who offered to take him in. They were a nice good-hearted group of young adults for the most part however, being a friend of someone with schizophrenia and living with someone with mental illness is two different things.

Since Rich didn't always have insurance and couldn't get any, because Medicaid is so overly strapped, he wasn't getting a lot of help he needed. So, Lake County Community Mental Health set Rich up with a case worker to help Rich with the adjustment to semi-independence. His case worker realized the challenges Rich faced but tried to be of help. She requested that while his friends were at work that he spent his time at the Monty J. Shone Community Center. This was a center for people with various disabilities. Since he was much more functional than many of their other clients, he was put to work doing janitorial work. This helped his self-esteem and gave him a real sense of accomplishment, while at the same time there were people around to watch out for him.

When he was working Rich stayed out of trouble. However, when he was left alone in the apartment often trouble would find him. Rich and his roommates had an agreement. They knew Rich often had delusions that distracted him from his daily tasks. They agreed that Rich would not do any major cooking that required him to use the oven.

One night all his roommates had other tasks to attend to so they were not home for dinner. So, they left a can of soup for Rich to heat up. The problem was as soon as he had opened the soup and started heating it up, "Him" decided to show up and halt Rich. "Him" attacked Rich so much that he forgot about his soup. When the first of Rich's roommates came home, he found a pan burned away with a flame still burning and Rich in a fetal position. When the other friends came home, they talked about what had happened.

James (the friend who found him curled up in the fetal position) said, "I love the guy but if we can't leave him alone for a couple of hours without worrying, he might burn the place down he is too much work for us to handle. Can't we check him into a mental institution? Amanda (the only woman living in this apartment) said, "I understand your point of view. In the past that might have been an option nonetheless, they do not exist anymore. Rich needs us, we will just have to arrange our schedules better."

Amanda was willing to give up her time if James gave in and let Rich stay. From that point on James and Amanda never left Rich home alone. Either James or Amanda were always with Rich even though they had lives of their own to live. James knew that his friend could not be left home alone because, Rich's actions were becoming stranger and stranger by the day. James loved Rich like a brother but, he worried that Rich's issues were too big for him and Amanda to deal with. He no longer was just seeing the "Lady in the White Dress" and "Him," he was becoming them. If this wasn't bad enough, Rich became injured at work. Rich had to come in late one day because he had to take care of some business related to his Disability insurance at the Social Security office. He had told his supervisor that he would be at work by 10a.m. Nevertheless, as life always goes things never go smooth when you are in a hurry. It took Rich longer to take care of his business than he expected so he missed his ride. Therefore, he had to call for another ride to work. By the time, he got to work it was after 11a.m. So, he was running to his post. The person who was covering for Rich forgot to put up a wet floor sign so when he came in, he was running. Because he was in a hurry to get to work. However, the person who was covering for him wasn't as diligent and careful as he always was about doing the janitorial work correctly. This person forgot to set out a "careful wet floor" sign. When Rich reached the wet spot, he slid. At first, Rich said, I'm fine." However, everyone could see that at the rate he hit the hall wall there was no way he was ok. They insisted that Rich go to the ER.

One of the CMH (community mental health) staff drove him to the ER. The doctors checked him out and said that he had broken one knee, twisted the other ankle, and got a minor head concussion. Therefore, the community center told him to take some time off and, that he could come back after it was healed. That was a nice ideal, if only it was true. As a nonprofit, the community center had to replace Rich so when Rich returned despite what he was told his job was filled.

Rich continued to spend his days at the community center. Even though the community center was set up to help those with mental and physical issues Rich could sense that the center was becoming uncomfortable with his worsening symptoms, and they were becoming concerned about the safety of the other clients. They both agreed that it was best if Rich stop attending the center.

Two Years Ago

His symptom started to get worse. When the Lady in the White Dress came, he wasn't just seeing her as before, he was becoming her. His voice sounded light and feminine and he acted like an angelic woman. When he became "Him" he acted and sounded like the evillest crazed man you could ever imagine.

Hearing these voices left James with only one thought, my friend is demon possessed. The truth was even though, the force of evil can and does terrorize people (and even possesses some people). Rich's friends did not truly know for sure that their friend was possessed. 87 However, when Him took over Rich he acted like the demon possessed people James saw in the movies.

James wasn't quite sure how to cast out a demon nevertheless, he knew Jesus said something about prayer and fasting. He informed Amanda of what he was trying to do. She thought it was pointless and insulting but she was willing to try anything to help her friend. So they both fasted. She wasn't about to let James do anything to Rich without her there, to protect Rich.

A week later, James performed the exorcism. James was disappointed that very little happened but for a while Rich was Rich. That is until the voices returned. Rich's delusions stayed away for several weeks yet, when they returned, they were stronger than ever. Amanda and James felt like they could leave Rich home alone now. But when Amanda came home from her date with her boyfriend Chuck, she found the apartment was a wreck. Couch cushions were torn apart, book shelfs broken with the books strewn all over the place. She yelled down the stairs for Chuck to come back, "Chuck come back, I need your help! Rich is having….!" Then she was knocked unconscious, Rich had hit her over the head with a shelf. He thought she was the lady in the white dress.

Chuck knew it was an accident for he was, aware of his girlfriend's schizophrenic roommate. However, right now it was not the time to think, it was time to act. Chuck wrestled the crazed man to the ground and shoved him into a bedroom, he locked the door. Then he called 911 about his girlfriend. When the EMTs came, they told Chuck that Amanda should be ok but they took her to the hospital just to be medically checked.

When James returned home, he was furious. As soon as Rich realized what he had done, he felt terrible. He knew that he had nearly killed one of his best friends. She was the only woman (besides his own mother) that ever stood up for him. As a result, before James could say a word, Rich said, "Listen to me! I'm so sorry!" Rich was weeping very hard but James said, "Rich, sorry isn't good enough, you are dangerous!" Rich interrupted him and said, "Yes I know, that is why I'm leaving." James said, "I think that would be best." So, Rich just left and never looked back.

This Past Winter

Steve Palmer was driving home from visiting his friend and discipling Skull Daniels. As he was driving home, he saw a homeless man holding up a sign it said, "Help me PLEASE! I'm homeless!" Steve had no idea of how he could help but he sensed he was supposed to stop so he did.

Steve said, "I'm heading home and I haven't had any dinner. Would you like to join me? I'll buy your meal." They stopped at a local Diner. While they waited for their meal to come, Steve asked this person his name. He said his name was Rich then he told Steve about how he had gotten to this point in his life.

Steve was a very intelligent person and being in the ministry he knew very well how unjust our society can be still, this man's plight stumped him. Steve asked, not knowing what the answer could be, "Can't you get Medicaid?" Rich said, "Everyone asks me that. No, I'm too young and I'm not a pregnant woman. Yes, children and the elderly need help but, what about people like me?" Steve said, "Huh? Medicaid is supposed to help low-income people and you can't get lower income than homelessness." Rich replied, "That was true in the old days yet today so many people are low-income and would qualify for Medicaid but the system can't handle them all. As the two men's meals were coming Steve said, "I can't do much but, I can give you a ride to a shelter. The nearest shelters were in Cadillac and Traverse City. Found out that the one in Traverse City had a bed available and therefore, Steve drove him there.

When they reached the New Hope Rescue Mission, Steve helped Rich check in and introduced him to Don Qusack the check in manage. Steve had informed them that Rich had mental health issues yet, the shelter was unaware of Rich's Schizophrenia and the severity to which it affected him. Therefore, when they interviewed him, when checking him in, Don became nervous. He really wanted to help Rich yet, he was not sure if they could safely accept him into their program. It just so happened that, Emma Murry (A social worker that worked with this mission) was there that day checking on a client. So, Mr. Qusack called her over to see if she could do anything to help Rich. She said, "Well I don't want to get anyone's hopes up but, I might have an idea. If Mr. Smith can pass a background check there is a group home just down the road I might be able to get him into. It is just opening and there are still a few slots available. It will only cost you around $800/month but LORD willing we should be able to either have disability or your insurance pay from it. However, that means we need to get busy today filling out the paperwork. Rich responded, "I have both. I have not been homeless very long. I would have tried to get into a group home before now if anyone had mentioned it before now but the topic just never came up."

So, Ms. Murry began the process of getting him into this group home. The first thing Rich had to do was sign a medical release form and a whole lot of other papers. After a brief time, Rich was called in for an in-take assessment. At this meeting, him and a case worker talked about what his needs were. They were pleased that he was so independent and still they 90 were able to create a plan for when he did have an incident. Since he was so independent. He would do many of his own task but a staff member would always be near in case something happened. Of course, he was required to take his medicine Nevertheless, in the long run, Rich ended up having more independence than he had ever had.

Discussion Questions

1. When you see a homeless person, what comes to mind about that person? What should be our attitude regarding the homeless? (Mathew 8:20, Mathew 25:31-46)

2. What is truly the most effective way you can help a person dealing with mental illness?

3. What's the difference between demon possession and mental illness?

4. What can you personally do to help the poor?

Chapter 17

Many times, Satan our enemy, is described to us by the world as a monster with horns and a pitchfork who is dressed in red. But, as anyone with half a brain knows this image is incorrect. The Bible describes the devil as an angel of light and the Accuser of the brethren. What's the most frightening thing of all, is his favorite agents of destruction, are us. The very people who say we have committed our lives to God, his enemy. Lucifer doesn't want you to know this but, it's true. Reader, if you are asking, how is Satan using my church and I? Well let me tell you a story, that is repeated each Sunday in thousands, tens of thousands, hundreds of thousands of times maybe even millions of times across the world.

Adam White was head of the Midwest division of the whole station Inc. Whole station is a major commercial radio network that has stations across the country. His company was building a new 50,000-Watt station in a Hartlin field that would be heard across all northern Michigan. However, there were several problems. There were equipment problems, problems with staff and of course problems with money. If anything could go wrong it did. Adam always tried to be in town as his new stations were about to launch to troubleshoot yet, he felt these problems were almost too much.

After a long Saturday night of troubleshooting, he found a church to attend yet, after working all night he looked like a wreck and he didn't have time to freshen up. When he walked in the door of

St. Thomas Church, he looked and smelled like a bum. Adam wished he could have freshened up more however, with everything going on it was hard enough making time to attend church much less find a time to dress up. Besides, he thought God doesn't care what he looked like.

When he walked in the door, he was glad to see that he wasn't swarmed by people like sharks to chum. Nevertheless, Adam was surprised no one even said a word to him. Everyone just stared at how shabby he looked and stayed in their own comfortable Cliques. Even, the Mitchell family who normally were very warm and welcoming to newcomers didn't seem to notice Adam.

Adam asked several people where the offering box was and nobody knew what he was talking about, so they gave him a look and said, "what are you talking about, crazy old man?" he pulled out his smart phone but, he couldn't find a website for St. Thomas Church in Hartlin, Michigan. When the plate was passed, Adam was not ready so he just tried to give it to his home church, back in Illinois. When he did this in older lady said, "Young man put that infuriated gadget away. Aren't you rather old to be playing in church?" Adam wanted to explain that he was just paying his tithe and that he also had his Bible on his smart phone. However, it wasn't worth fighting about, so he put his phone away. When the plate came to him the usher shook it, to indicate that he was supposed to give something. Adam just shook his head and said, "No thank you." Afterwards, Adam noticed people were looking at him.

Pastor Palmer preached from James 2 about how we shouldn't show favoritism. After hearing this passage those sitting near Adam, who had looked down on him, felt extremely guilty. The very thing James spoke against was what they were doing. They thought, "What if he is too poor to own "proper" church clothing or to give his tithe?"

Samantha who had neglected welcoming Adam whisper to her husband, "Michael I sense we need to invite the visitor to lunch." After service Michael caught up with Adam before he left and said, "Hello, I am Michael Mitchell and this is my lovely wife Samantha and our children Amber, Jason and Gregory. And you are?" Adam said, "My name is Adam White." The Mitchells said "nice to meet you, Adam. We would like to invite you to lunch, don't worry we will pay." Adam said, "you really don't need to I'm actually quite well off." But Samantha said, "Well we insist anyway."

Adam accepted the invitation while they waited for their meal to arrive, he told the Mitchell's about his busy life. Hearing his story in knowing how their church had treated Adam they felt just awful. Michael and Samantha apologized on behalf of their church. Adam said, "That is okay, to be honest, I hate to admit it, but I probably would do the same thing you did, if I was in your shoes." Michael said, "No it is not okay, just because we are naturally prejudice people doesn't mean we should be okay with it. Jesus was not prejudice, neither should we. 95

Discussion Questions

1. In what ways does Satan use people who claim to be Christians? (1 Corinthians 13:1-7, James 2:1-4, 14-20, Matthew 25:31-46)

2. How does your church treat visitors who may not dressed in their Sunday best? How do you treat visitors?

3. How are we supposed to treat visitors to our fellowship? (Luke 10:25-37, James 2:1-9, 14-17)

4. What can you and your congregation do to be more Christ like to the people you encounter?

Chapter 18

The topic of this topic chapter may be the most controversial chapter in this book. You might think: "I don't need to read, these people are not in my church" The truth is they may be in your church, but they are keeping this part of their lives secret from you, or they are not a part of your church, but they ought to be.

This chapter is dealing with Lesbian, Gay, Bisexual and Transgendered (LGBT) people. Before we begin let me lay out some facts. If you disagree with me, please do your own research. Search the Scriptures. Do not take my word, or the words of your pastor as the final authority, that honor belongs to God. (Acts 17:11)

Fact 1

God loves all people, and wishes that, "everyone would come to repentance" 2 Peter 3:9

Fact 2

God hates all forms of sexual immorality, both homosexual and heterosexual immorality equally both are sinful in God's eyes. Romans 6:23

Fact 3

There is a difference between being something and doing something.

Because the Bible does forbid homosexual acts, and because people are uncomfortable with LGBT people, many churches have condemned those who struggle with LGBT feelings, even when they have never acted upon the feelings. These churches fail to be Jesus to these hurting people.

Modern Day

Most people at St. Thomas Church didn't worry about LGBT people. They thought this was just a big city problem and/or they simply did not know what this was. However, for two young men who were loved and respected members of St. Thomas Church it was an everyday struggle. It was a personal struggle and, they feared that others in the church would discover they were that "thing" that others in the church feared.

Buck McDonald was born to two loving parents. He grew up in a strict conservative Christian family. When other young men started noticing young ladies; he could not help being attracted to other boys.

He feared these feelings and hated himself for lusting after members of his own sex. He knew that acting on these feelings would be sin, so he did all he could to give the illusion that he was straight. He dated girls in high school and college. Then he married the first girl to say, "Yes." He tried to deny that he was gay, yet he could not stop being attracted to other men. So, a few times a year he would travel to Cadillac. He did not go to cheat on his wife. He loved her and was faithful to her. Yet, he was not sexually attracted to his wife. He went to Cadillac to be around others who had similar struggles.

Tonight, he was surprised to see somebody he knew from his everyday life. "She" walked in with the clumsy strut of a man. It was clear she was not really a woman. Buck would not have paid much attention to her, but she looked familiar. Who was she?" Buck thought. This "woman" had the same thoughts in her head; however, she had a little more nerve. So, she walked up to Buck and said,

"Buck Mc Donald, what are you doing here?" "I was wondering the same thing", said Buck, then he replied, "Robin, what are you, a church elder doing here, dressed as a woman?"

As with Buck, Robin Richards grew up in a conservative Christian family, in a small town. The only time he heard any talk about transgendered people was when they were talked about in cruel jokes. He had no idea what it meant to be transgendered, all he knew was that he did not feel normal. As he grew up, he enjoyed dressing up like a girl. He understood himself only a little better as he became older. As a teenager, he became envious of female peers that developed mature female physical attributes. He felt that his body was betraying him. He loved the Lord however, he struggled with unhappiness over being born with a body that did not reflect the gender he felt he should be.

Robin felt a call to ministry, so that is the career he pursued. In college, he dated many women. He felt that it would not be right to marry any of them, and force them to deal with his issues. He did find a job as an associate pastor. When he did not express normal heterosexual attraction, people suspected his struggle with gender identity issues, he was dismissed. He feared that this pattern would be repeated in any other churches, in which he tried to minister so, he got a job as a truck driver.

When he found St. Thomas Church, he knew he had found a place to call home, and to receive a fresh start. After he had been in the church for a while, his faith and experience in church administration, caused him to be asked to be an elder. He kept his transgender struggles secret.

When Buck and Robin saw each other at the gay bar, they were embarrassed, but it quickly turned to relief. They now had another person to share their struggles with. When Buck saw Robin, dressed as a woman, he said "Robin Richards, what are you doing dressed like…" Robin said "It is true. I am transgendered. What about you, Buck?" Buck replied nervously, 99

"I'm, ah not sure how to put it. I'm uh gay… But I don't want to be. I try to like women; but men are so handsome!" Then he broke down crying and said, "Why does God hate me, so much?" Robin tried to comfort Buck by saying, "Listen, God loves you. The Bible repeatedly states that God loves ALL people, even though we are dirty rotten sinners"

He loves all people, and that includes us. Remember God will not put us through more than we can handle through Him. Then Buck replied, "so what are you saying? Should we just go out and live up our LGBT lifestyle?" "No! As Paul said in chapter six of Romans we are dead to sin, that old sin nature may keep on trying to drag us back, into slavery but we must not let it. Since Pentecost we have been living in the new kingdom and have the Holy Spirit to help us follow Christ nevertheless, all mankind has weaknesses. When Christ returns, these weaknesses will be removed." replied Robin.

Reader, it may seem I ended the chapter too abruptly, yet I feel I have made my point. I am not saying that homosexual activity and transgenderism should be treated as normal. The Bible clearly states that homosexual activity is sin. What I am saying is that we should have empathy and understanding for those that struggle with LGBT issues even, if this is something you don't struggle with. We all have struggles, whether it is the one just discussed or something more acceptable to the world and/or the church, such as gossip or greed. Any sin left unchecked will destroy your relationship with the Lord.

We as the church should never be ok with sin. God does not have degrees of sin. All sin including this that might seem small in our eyes is worthy of death. The church should be a welcoming place, where people can be honest about their struggles. Only then, can they find healing from the only one that can heal completely, Jesus Christ.

<h1 style="text-align:center">Discussion Questions</h1>

1. What would you do if you were Buck or Robin? Would you go to a gay bar? Should you seek out others that share your struggles, or not?

2. Should you marry if you know you have a serious personal problem? What about cases like the one talked about in I Cor.7:9 But if they cannot control themselves, they should marry, for it is better to marry than to burn with passion.

3. How should we act toward members in our fellowship that are struggling with LGBT issues? Does it matter if they are practicing? If so, why? (Eph. 5:3) Do you have someone you can share your struggles with? If so, what is the benefit of having this person in your life? What if any harm can this person cause?

4. Does God really hate someone because they struggle with LGBT?

5. We all have heard the stories of people set free from various addiction(s). What should our reaction be if freedom from whatever our personal addiction, does not come easy? (2 Corinthians 12: 6-10)

Chapter 19

Nick Clyne was a nice guy who loved helping people. This was probably why he became a history teacher. Every day he went to work and saw his students learning to love the past more than the day before was a great joy to him. But then it happened the day that would change his life forever.

It started out like any other day. He took attendance. As soon as he called Kate Calkins she reacted to him like a viper on the attack so, he tried to give her space yet he couldn't just let her disrupt the classroom. On his way to help another student, Kate stood up, to go talk to another girl, thus Nick bumped into her. He told her to sit down. Then he went to help another student who needed help.

When Nick got back to his desk Kate gave her teacher a dirty look that Mr. Clyne took to mean quotation your dead, I'm going to get you." Until that moment he pretty much ignored Kate figuring she was just having a bad day. However, from that moment on he couldn't stop worrying, knowing that even a small phony accusation would end his career. The next day, on his way to his class the principal informed him that he has been suspended because a student accused him of inappropriate touching. Nick said, "I only brushed past Miss Calkins. At that point he was informed that it was not Miss Calkins that made the accusation. This left Nick completely baffled. He knew he was innocent nevertheless; with this kind of case he knew his career was over.

Nick felt a mixture of emotions, anger that someone would accuse him of doing something so heinous. Scared as to how he was going to survive. Yet, at the same time Nick felt compassion for the student who accused him of touching her. He didn't know what has gone on in her life that would lead her to suspect a teacher of having improper motives.

When news reached his church, they asked him to leave. They loved him and wish they could support him, but too many parents (even these who knew him well) felt uncomfortable with an accused sex offender around their children.

Nick Clyne was Edna's youngest son. He didn't want to tell his mother about the sad and embarrassing development in his life. He figured his mother would over react to this information. He was surprised but, she didn't worry too much about this and was just supportive. When he told her about what happened she just asked how could she help him? He said, "Well, mom please pray for me. His mother said, "Of course I will." Then she said, "let's do it now." So, they held hands and prayed. "Father God you are so good to us yet we are so fickle. When trouble comes, we tend to run. Please forgive us for our lack of faith and please help us to trust you for the bright beautiful future that you have promised us. Future with the lover of our souls. We are so weak. We do not see past our own feet but, you see the whole picture past, present and future

Please help us to see our situation with your eyes. We are needy people who need your help now. Please have your will. Help Nick to trust you no matter what he must go through in the future. In the name of your holy son Jesus Christ amen. "

I'm sure you will be welcome anytime at St. Thomas." Said, Nick's mother. Nick wasn't so sure about how well he would be accepted at his childhood church. If New New Deli Wesleyan church (the church he had been attending) wouldn't accept him what chance was there, that St. Thomas Church would accept him. But they did accept him. He didn't bring it up to most people. Yet, anyone who watch the news could have heard what was going on with him.

His case was weighing so heavily on him at times he even questioned if everybody's life would be better off if he was out of the picture. You knew how wrong these feelings were yet, he felt powerless to stop these feelings. However, he met great prayer warriors who sensed his feeling and who prayed nonstop with and for him.

These prayers were needed because he had no idea what he was doing and why the system was against him. He was forced to plead no contest. Which meant his career was over but people at his church helped him find a new job. The road to come was rough but, with the support of his church and family his life worked out fine.

Discussion Questions

1. What would you do if you discovered there was a sex offender at your church? How would you want people to treat you if you were accused of criminal sexual conduct? How does the Bible say you should treat them? (Ephesians 5)

2. Is there ever a time when it is okay to ask someone to leave your church? (1 Corinthians 5)

3. When bad things happen in your life should you share the news with your loved ones, why and under what criteria? (Galatians 6:2, James 5:16, 2 Corinthians 1:7)

4. How can you personally support people in crisis? (Galatians 6:2)

5. We all have heard the stories of people set free from various addiction(s). What should our reaction be if freedom from whatever our personal addiction, does not come easy? (2 Corinthians 12: 6-10)

Chapter 20

Steve Palmer was loved by his flock. When he first came to St. Thomas Church he was thought of as a kid. The younger members of the congregation enjoyed having someone close to their own age leading them but, the older people felt odd having a new younger person pastoring their church. Steve Palmer was only the third pastor to ever lead St. Thomas Church.

However, Pastor Palmer's kindness, wisdom and heart for outreach won everyone over. But there was a downside. The people of St. Thomas Church came to him with all their problems including issues that could and should have been dealt with in their small group.

Thirty Years Ago

Jed Gray was a humble God-fearing man. His family had been following the LORD longer than anyone could track. Some might say, "I'm a Christian because I grew up in the church. Which as we know growing up going to church isn't enough to make you a Christ follower, you must purposely and intentionally choose Jesus as your personal God and Savior. In Jed's case, he did choose to follow Jesus and he kept following Jesus all his life. Jed's younger brother Eddie on the other hand grew up in the same household and started out following Christ however, he just could not get past the hypocrisy he saw. So-called Christians, who would praise God on Sunday then on Monday hurt their neighbor with no mercy. Thus, Eddie turned his back on God and just became increasingly hard hearted toward God.

One Week Ago

Jed was in his small group. At prayer time, he broke down crying, "My little brother Eddie wants nothing to do with God. He is in the hospital and the doctors say he could die at any time now. Please pray that he will choose God before he passes." Another member of the group 106 asked, "Have you asked Pastor Palmer to go talk to Eddie? It's Pastor Palmer's job anyway." Something about this didn't sound quite right nevertheless, he was desperate so, he figured he better try asking his pastor.

Modern Day

Carissa, Steve Palmer secretary knocked on his study door and said, "Pastor are you busy? There is a Mr. Gray here to see you. Pastor Palmer said, "I am busy but send him in anyways."

Mr. Gray walked in looking meek and depressed. He said, "Pastor, I don't mean to disturb you but my small group and I humbly request that you come and visit my brother who is in the hospital and the doctors don't think he has much more time to live." Steve asked, "why do you want me to visit him? You are the ones who know him best." Mr. Grey smiled and said, "Pastor isn't visiting the sick part of your job, you are the minister." Steve wanted to respond by saying, "No, I'm the pastor it's my job to equip you to do things just like this, it is your job to visit the sick!" Yet, Steve knew it wasn't worth making a big deal over so he went to see Mr. Gray's brother.

When Pastor Palmer got to the hospital, he knocked on the door and said, "Eddie, Eddie grey? I am…" Eddie, who was very cranky interrupted him and said, "I know who the hell you are; you are that fucking Pastor, from that motherfucking church of his. If the fucking rat bastard brother of mine thinks just because he had some goody goody know it all pastor come to see me on my deathbed that I'm going to get saved he's got another thing coming."

Steve listen to this angry man verbally rundown God and Christianity and finally he had enough and Pastor Palmer ranted, "Mr. Gray that's enough, I don't care what you say about me or my church, just don't rag on my God! God loves you and your brother loves you! Admittedly, asking me to talk to you about God was a very cowardly move but, his motives were good. Eddie, I don't care if your life sucked and that you were screwed over more times than you can count! If the doctors are right, tonight you will stand before God and you will have to answer for the crimes you committed in this life."

Eddie responded, "I ain't no criminal!" Pastor Palmer responded, "During our talk you blasted profanity and you kept using God's name in vain. That alone makes you worthy of Hell since God said, "Do not use the name of the Lord your God in vain." He responded, "then I have nothing to fear because he is not my God." Pastor Palmer said, "then you choose hell." Eddie said "In a sarcastic tone, great all my best friends are there and there is none of those religious hypocritical nuts. Pastor Palmer exclaimed, "You are dead wrong it is a place of pain and agony beyond anything we can imagine and it goes on forever!" Eddie shouted "BS!" When I'm gone, I'm gone. And with that he was dead. Steve couldn't get through to this man that he was needlessly choosing damnation. Pastor Palmer felt like a failure.

Discussion Questions

1. If growing up going to church doesn't make you a Christ follower what does? (Romans 10:9)

2. Since we are saved by faith why should our works matter? (James 2:14-19)

3. Just what is the role of a pastor and/or elders? (1 Timothy 3:1-13, Acts 6:1-7)

4. If this is the role of a pastor why do we, the church, tend to add on other responsibilities that we could and should be doing ourselves?

5. How can we be so sure that there is a heaven waiting for us on the other side? (1 Thessalonians 4:13-17, John 14:1-2)

6. Are you a failure if you fail to convince someone to accept the Lord as their Savior? (1 Corinthians 3:6, Romans 9:5-18)

Chapter 21

New New Deli Wesleyan church for many years was the largest church in the small town of New New Deli, Michigan. Yet, over time they started to lose members. First, they lost their members from Hartlin. They figured, "Okay, that's fine, those people are just old country bumpkins anyway." However, they were not the last to leave, many more people left.

As the years passed, new churches sprung up. No matter how the community changed New New Deli Wesleyan church remained the same. The core members liked things the way they were, and were unwilling to change. Even though, their stubbornness was slowly killing their church.

Their elders knew this was not the way things should be so, they agreed to pray and fast to seek God's will. After fasting for a week, they all agreed to ask their estranged daughter church for help. The elders knew that many on the Church Council still held resentment that the "rebels", as they were called by those who were old enough to remember the exodus of the Hartlin members. Yet, the elders were positive that God was commanding them, to ask St. Thomas Church for help staying afloat. Harold Nixon was assigned to tell the board what the elders were sensing to be God's will. As he expected the elders' decision led to disagreement. "my great-great-grandfather pastored at this church when those deserters left. Just because we wouldn't help them start their own church, they ran off and started a church anyway." Nathan Kelly said; We didn't have problems before they left, in fact they are probably the cause of all our troubles! Why should we ask those rebels to help us?" Harold said "because God said so." Nathan replied "we wouldn't help them a century ago, why should they help us now?" The abandonment issues of the older members of the board were acknowledged but, enough of the board had to admit the elders were right. Forgiving St. Thomas Church and asking them for help clearly was in line with what God would want. So, they contacted Pastor Palmer and the rest of their leadership team.

"Hello Pastor Palmer I'm Scott Warren, I'm the senior pastor of the New New Deli Wesleyan church. We need your advice."

Pastor Palmer was surprised. Pastor Palmer was a rather young man in his early 30s and an extremely inexperienced pastor. What could he know that, Pastor Warren who was in his mid-50s did not know? Pastor Warren said, "Pastor Palmer you may be young, and you may pastor a small church. However, your church is healthy and at least it is reaching out to your community and it is growing. My church is very stagnant and it is dying. My people refuse to look past themselves and do what is needed to reach their community. Many of the older people in our church refuse to forgive your church for leaving us and that was nearly a century ago." Pastor Palmer said, "If we can't get them to love and forgive their brothers in Christ they will not be able to reach those who don't know Jesus. So how about we have a picnic where our two churches can come together. We can do it at Tuttle Oak Park, which would be about equal distance between our two churches. How about the last Saturday of next month?" Pastor Warren said, "that sounds good."

The young people of New New Deli Wesleyan church who usually didn't care for picnics were the people who were the most excited about the picnic. They were excited because it was something new. But, they were not the ones Pastor Warren was the most concerned about. This gathering was supposed to be the first step in trying to reconnect their church and St. Thomas Church. Pastor Warren wasn't sure how he was going to convince the angry older people to attend. All he could do was plead that everyone attend. So only out of loyalty to their pastor did people, including the most reluctant elderly people attend.

At St. Thomas Church, Pastor Palmer had the same problem for different reasons. Some of those who have come since its founding had left New New Deli Wesleyan church, and for these people their discomfort was often because of personal conflicts and other dirty little secrets. Forgiveness was not their motive, it was fear. Fear that they would be exposed.

Nick Clyne who was among those with secrets pulled his pastor aside and said, "Pastor do you realize that by forcing people to interact with that church many people like myself fear their baggage will be dug up? Pastor your motives are good yet, you may be opening a dumpster of worms." Pastor Palmer answered Nick's objections with, "I understand what you are saying but you should not fear your secrets coming out none of us have a reason to judge for we all have things in our past we are not proud of. Some people's past may seem worse than others by human standards but, all have fallen short of God's standards and he is the person we ultimately need to answer to." Nick knew this truth nevertheless; it wasn't much help he was still scared.

Pastor Palmer knew that there were others with the same fears Nick had. Consequently, that same day he addressed the congregation with the issue. He began his message with these words, "it has been brought to my attention that some of you have things about your past you would rather not be known to others around you. Well, I would like to argue that you are not abnormal. We read about a time when the teachers of religious law and Pharisee tried to trick Jesus by bringing an adulterous woman before Jesus. But in the end, he shut them up by saying "alright, but let the one who has never sinned throw the first stone! In the end, everybody slowly walked away for even the most righteous person there (not including Jesus) had to admit, in one way or another they too had sinned at some point in their life. So, I want each and every one of you to promise me no matter how juicy the dirt you hear about your brothers and/or sisters, keep it to yourself and don't hold it against them." One by one commitments were made to keep secret about all the rumors they would hear about their fellow believers.

The Saturday of the picnic came. The pastors and leaders of these two churches stood there wondering if this experiment was going to work or totally blow up in their faces. But just as they were starting to worry cars started pulling up from two different sides of the park.

The rainbow of people from various backgrounds caused these two pastors to feel both anxiety and tranquility at the same time. They felt anxious for they didn't know how such different people would get along. Tranquility for this is what the kingdom is about, different kinds of people coming together under the one banner of Christ.

An older lady from New New Deli laid down her dirt pudding just as Jenna and Bud Newcomb who were from St. Thomas we're sitting down with their taco salad. Jenna was covered with piercings. Despite being well in her 20s she looked to her New New Deli counterparts to be no more than 15 years of age. The older woman said, "young lady, how could your mother allow you to mutilate your body?" Jenna said, "Pardon me, I am a 28-year-old married woman with a baby on the way! So, it's not exactly any of her business what I do with my body. However, she doesn't have a problem with my piercings."

After calming down Jenna said, "hey you make dirt pudding exactly like my mom makes her's. Just as she was saying this Jenna's mother put her dirt pudding down. Jenna couldn't help but notice they were identical. Jenna said, "Where did you get your recipe?" Then her mother said, "I learned from my great aunt Marlene." The older woman said, "I used my mother's recipe." The younger woman asked, "What is your mother's name?" These two women discovered they were distant cousins.

This wasn't the only thing these two groups found they had in common. Edna from St. Thomas and Agnes from New New Deli found they both hated the way things change so quickly these days. However, Agnes couldn't help but ask, "Some of our young people say, it's our unwillingness to change that got us in trouble. Yet, you Edna seem as old-fashioned as I am, so if being unwilling to change doesn't kill a church, what does?" Edna replied, "This hasn't been an easy lesson for me, I've had to learn that I kill the church. If I care more about what I want and what makes me feel comfortable than loving God and truly loving other people, the church can't grow and when it stops growing it dies. Remember what Jesus said, "I am the true vine, and my father is the gardener he cuts off every branch in me that bears no fruit." (John 15:1-2b) *This was a hard lesson for me to learn. I grew up believing people should stay with their own kind. But God loves us all the same so, segregation is not his way.

Please don't get me wrong there is a place for old time religion. God can and does use us and our gifts right where we are. We must be open to God and willing to love people the same way Jesus does." Agnes said, "Yes, well I do that." Edna said, "I thought I too was doing that but, I discovered there was still more I could do."

Bud sat down at the end of a picnic table and started strumming some praise choruses. William Jamison a stuffy looking man from New New Deli saw Bud playing his guitar and said, "That sounds lovely whatta playing?" Bud said, "I'm just strumming some praise choruses. As it is, my old lady didn't want me to bring it nevertheless, I thought why not? William responded, "My wife can be a drag sometimes yet, I respect her wishes. I maybe the head of my family but, I am to love her and I know when I'm embarrassing her that is not showing love." Bud didn't like hearing this but he knew William was right. Yet, he couldn't help feeling like William was being 114 holier than Thou.

William said, "I like your playing." Bud said, "Well I get plenty of practice. I play in the worship band at church and at small group. William said, "I'm so jealous at my church all we play is hymns played on piano and organ. We never sing anything with a beat." Bud said, "I don't think you understand, we sing hymns at St. Thomas our hymns just have a fuller sound because we use other instruments besides piano."

"Can you believe the nerve of Christ Assemblies of God, asking if we wanted to do some community worship services with them and some other churches?" Said Agnes. Edna said, "What is so bad about doing a community unity service with other churches? I think you would find it to be a very beautiful and meaningful service. Agnes said, "Wash your mouth out with soap!"

We are Wesleyans; we don't associate with Pentecostals! The Pentecostals are our competition. The only reason we agreed to work with your church is you clearly are doing something right since you were growing, and even though, you no longer consider yourself Wesleyans you came from us." Edna replied, "Madam, I respectfully disagree." Jesus said, "Anyone who is not against us is with us." Agnes wanted to argue this point but, she couldn't for she knew Edna was right.

When nearly everyone had shown up, the two pastors walked to the front of the pavilion. Pastor Palmer welcomed everyone and said, "Welcome everyone I'm so glad our two churches could come together and learn from each other." Several people from New New Deli murmured, "learn from each other, St. Thomas Church don't you mean indoctrinate us into your way of doing things."

Samantha Mitchell heard what some people from New New Deli Wesleyan church were saying and she said, "No, we from St. Thomas Church can learn a lot from you." One person in the crowd responded, what can you learn from us!" Samantha responded to their sarcasm with love and said, "You have a wonderful senior ministry and you are good at guarding yourself from worldly influences. You may go overboard sometimes yet, we at times can be too lax. You should do what you are good at, this is where the Lord has gifted you. Still, at the same time you need to be open to change with the needs of the community however, not at the expense of the truth."

Discussion Questions

1. How can we be sure of what God's will is?

2. Why must we forgive those who have offended us? (Matthew 18:21-35, Matthew 6: 12-15, Mark 11:25, Luke 6:37

3. Why shouldn't we judge or fear judgment from fellow believers? (Luke 6:37, John 1-11, Matthew 7:1, Romans 3:1-6, 1 Corinthians 4:3, Colossian 2: 16, James 4: 11)

4. What can you learn from people older than yourself? What can you learn from people younger than yourself? (1 Timothy 5, Titus 2:1-8)

Chapter 22

Steve Palmer was a very kind hearted godly man, who felt very honored to be called a pastor. He truly wanted to be a good example to his congregation. To the outside world, he projected the image of a fearless man of God yet, inside he was nervous and the enemy was about to feast on his emotions.

His flock loved him. For Steve gave them plenty of attention. Steve loved his people more than he loved himself. He knew he was no good to his people if he didn't take care of himself yet, he was driven to serve the Lord and the people that he was given even to the risk of his own health.

The deacons and elders saw the trouble that lay ahead for their pastor. Wilfred Waterford was assigned to approach Steve about the trouble they foresaw. Pastor, we as a church know how much you love us and we love you. In fact, we love you too much to let you keep going the way you are going. We as leaders of this church demand that you take some time off. Have you called Pastor Warren? You need to be mentored." Wilfred said   A self-righteous part of himself wanted to shout, "Pastor Scott Warren's church was dying before we taught them how to do church right. What can the Senior Pastor of New New Deli Wesleyan Church teach me!" but, pastor Palmer knew better than to listen to that voice so he reluctantly said, "no, I must admit, when Pastor Warren suggested that we should collaborate I thought what can we teach them. Now that we are teaching them I really don't know what Pastor Warren can teach me. Yet, I must admit I have become a dull knife in need of sharpening. I do need the guidance of one who has been doing this longer than I have."

Steve called pastor Warren. This is Steve Palmer from St Thomas Church in Hartland, it's been awhile since we talked but my church leaders are concerned that I'm not getting mentored. Pastor Warren had planned to go fishing and just have some alone time with God yet, he sensed that he needed to invite Steve along so he said, Steve you wouldn't happen to be free this weekend, would you? Steve replied, "actually, I am. My deacons are making me take some time off. Scott replied, then find a replacement, you and I are going fishing up at Long Lake this weekend."

Early Saturday morning Scott stops by Steve's house. Steve was still half asleep but, Scott said, "come on sleepy head it's time for you to go grab your stuff and jump in my truck." Steve thought he must be dreaming. It was so early and Scott's truck is so old and rusty that it was surprising that it was still running. On the way, up to Traverse City they stopped and bought some coffee.

On their way to the lake pastor Warren asked Steve about his ministry, "so how do you like being a pastor", Steve answered, "it's okay." Scott wouldn't let Steve get away with such a pat answer so he said, "come on pastor if you want me to mentor you, you gotta be honest with me, so really how has it been going?" Then Steve broke down, "it sucks! I had such big dreams. I wanted to come in and create a powerful army for Jesus. I thought being a pastor of the only church in the little village of Hartland, Michigan was going to be easy. However, I feel like I'm wasting my time! The saved are saved and the unsaved are unsaved. Families asked me to witness to their members as if I had some magic golden tongue that people couldn't help but come to the Lord when I spoke. This is such bull!

One man from my church asked me to visit his brother. Well, I visited this man's dying brother and when I did I discovered the sick man wanted nothing to do with me or God. So, no matter what I said this man refused to listen and, in the end, he died anyway without accepting the Lord! I feel like such a failure as a pastor."

Scott replied, "Steve you know very well that we are just messengers. If the person we deliver the truth to just crumples it up, throws it away and refuses to listen, we can pray that they respond before it is too late however, in the end the choice is between them and God." Steve then said, "but, it is too late now! This man died without choosing Christ." Scott asked, "Did you do everything you could to point this man to the truth?" Steve answered, "yes" "then you have nothing to feel guilty about" answered Scott. "Remember what the Apostle Paul said, 'I planted the seed, Apollos watered it, but God made it grow.' If you did your part in sharing the gospel, this man's rejection of the faith in Christ is out of your hands and you can't force another person to believe in Jesus."

Then Pastor Warren made a prophetic statement. "Pastor Steve Palmer you want to save the lost, don't you? You see yourself as a shepherd to those sheep. You want to hold their hand on every spiritual matter but, you can't. You are their leader and their teacher. However, if these baby birds are ever going to soar you gotta let them fall. I also bet you already have heard that you need to delegate. I know I am right because I was where you are now when I first started out as a pastor. It is natural to be and you need to be as passionate as you are now to ignite that passion in your people but, once the fire is lit you need to stand back and let it blaze. Otherwise, you will burn out."

When got to Pastor Warren's cabin, they unloaded their gear and went to the lake to start fishing. When they got out to the lake, Steve felt rather awkward that he hadn't done much fishing but, he wasn't going to argue with his mentor. So, he decided to just go with the flow. After some time on the water Scott said, "since we are already on the water I want to show you my special spot." Steve wasn't so sure what to make of this, so he said, "okay, whatever you say."

Reverend Warren turned his boat motor on to its lowest setting and headed for a small island in the middle of the lake. This made Steve a bit nervous. He couldn't help but think, "what in the world is this old man doing? We are going to get stuck in these weeds and what if this is just a clump of weed so there is no land to stand on? But there was land enough for two people and they didn't get stuck in the weeds."

Reverend Warren said, "Pastor Palmer we pastors are so used to ministering to others that many times we forget that we need to have time alone with God to be ministered to. Even, Jesus who was the son of God needed to have time alone with his father. So, that is what we are doing here. I will drop you off here for the next few hours and I want you to talk to God and I want you to take time to be quiet and to just listen for God to speak to you. I will come back for you later."

Pastor Steve Palmer presented himself as a brave man of God. A man who will do and/or say anything God tells him to say or do. But, when Steve is alone with God he isn't so brave. Pastor Warren was asking Steve to put a lot of faith in him, faith in a person he didn't know so well. However, Steve knew he had to trust this man. At first, he wasn't so sure what to say so he told God about his nervousness. After that subsided, he just sat there listening to the wind. Listening for some sign of God's voice. It wasn't long before he and God were communicating. Once this happened, time passed so quickly that it felt like minutes instead of the six hours which it had been.

On the way, back to the cabin Scott asked Steve what he thought of his time alone? Steve said, "well at first, I felt a mixture of fear and anxiety. Why would you leave me out in the middle of a lake and what do I say to God for several hours? Nevertheless, I turn my anxious thoughts 121 over to God and God challenged me about my workaholism and my need, to be my church's Savior, instead I need to direct them to the Savior.

Discussion Questions

1. Is it all right to take some time away from ministry? If so, why? (Mark 1:35-39, Mark 14:32-42, Luke 4:1-30)

2. Is it all right to confront a pastor about problems you see they may or may not, see?

3. What can we learn from more experienced Christians? Are you willing to listen to them?

4. Why do we expect so much from pastors and so little from ourselves?

5. Why is it so important to have alone time with God?

Chapter 23

Rev. Warren continue to mentor Steve. At first Steve found his mentor's guidance rather hard to follow and it was both too rigid and radical. The disciplines Rev. Warren stressed were hard to follow because it included fasting not only food but for whatever vice a person might care a little too much about at least one day a week. Vices such as TV, Internet and even driving. Scott Warren didn't ask Steve to fast. Steve, willingly fasted himself. Rev. Warren had walked in the same shoes as Pastor Palmer was currently walking in right now. He cried the same tears, stood on the same mountains, and fell off the same cliffs. Thus, Steve may have struggled to abide by his mentor's direction yet, he knew Scott knew from experience what was best. It wasn't that Rev. Warren was telling him to do the impossible or something Steve knew to be wrong. He knew that Scott loved him like a son. Yet, Steve felt like his spiritual father was dragging him up a hill he wasn't so sure if he was ready to climb.

If this wasn't bad enough, and 80-foot monster named Steve Palmer, all his sin nature, all his fears, and all the things the Father longed to skim off, sought with all its might to drag him down. Pastor Palmer agreed to be mentored because he was on the verge of burning out. Now he couldn't help but look at Rev. Warren and see how unworthy he was to preach the gospel. Scott could see the melancholy Steve was falling into and he would often say, do not compare yourself to me I am but a man like you. You should judge yourself by the standard of Christ. The standard that in this life is impossible to reach. However, do not let that drag you down for this life is a journey and it will take a lifetime to reach. Yet, it will be worth it when we get to the destination. Change is hard in fact; it is impossible in our own strength. It is only possible in the strength of our loving Father God.

Rev. Warren held some very radical ideas or at least ideas that would make some of his congregation a bit uncomfortable. He dared to be valuable to God and to be a trustworthy Christian friend. Steve knew that when he asked Rev. Warren to mentor him it was going to mean that he was going to have to be vulnerable. But, he never imagined that it was going to hurt this much.

Vulnerability as he was soon to discover hurts because when you are accountable to another person, you commit to change. Hence you give up the freedom to return to your old way of life. However, in the long run this is better for you because, you no longer run alone.

Discussion Questions

1. What is fasting and why is it important? (Isaiah 58)

2. Why is it important to practice what you preach to those under your authority? (1 Corinthians 11:1, 2 Corinthians 11:1-15, John 13:15, Philippians 3:17, 1 Timothy 4:12, Titus 2:7)

3. How can something you truly need become an idol? Why do these things have so much power over us? How do we realistically take away their power? (Luke 14:26-27, Matthew 6:19-34)

4. Why does it take strength to be vulnerable? Why must we be vulnerable to God and to another person? (Acts 2:42-42, Galatians 5:23, Ephesians 4:2, Colossians 3:12, 1 Timothy 6:11, Titus 3:2, James 1:21, James 3:13, Matthew 11:29, Matthew 21:5, 2 Corinthians 10:1)

5. Why is it better that God is walking with us in this journey? (Ephesian 1:1, Philippians 1:1, Colossians 1:2, 1 Thessalonians 4:16, John 16:5-16)

Chapter 24

The apostle Paul said, "the things I want to do I don't and the things I don't want to do I keep on doing, what a wretched man Am I." Worst of all, many of us who call ourselves followers of Christ know what we need to do to protect ourselves from temptation and/or the appearance of wrongdoing. Yet, we are too naïve to do it when the time of testing comes.

Pastor Palmer's popularity with his flock had become a serious problem. He tried to be nice and say, "please unless it is an emergency call before stopping by my office, however, after months of people abusing Pastor Palmer's kindness and Steve falling behind on his work, the church board decided he needed to lock the church doors during his office hours. This seemed like trouble waiting to happen to Steve, because during many of these same hours his secretary Carissa was the only person there at the church. One of the board members said, "Can't you just choose different office hours than her?" Steve said, "I wish we could yet, I need her around at least some of the time when I'm here."

Most of the church board said, "Pastor nothing is going to happen. You work with her all the time and nothing has happened, has it? Besides, you are a good godly man and she is practically your wife." Then Pastor Palmer ended the conversation by saying, "yes but she is not my wife."

At first everything was going well however, the first day Steve and Carissa had to work together locked in this building alone. This big empty church building caused Steve to feel odd, even scared. Carissa was a beautiful woman with blonde wavy hair. She was in her 20s with the figure of a supermodel however she was only average height. Steve was always told not to be alone with a woman and he felt like he was being forced to be alone with this woman.

Nothing happened at least for some time. This cause Steve to think maybe everything would be okay and that he was worrying about nothing. Satan is a patient little devil, who can and does wait if patients would allow him to bring down a well-respected believer. Locked in a prison; a prison which for most, serves as the Lord's house of worship, the enemy could use, to destroy both Pastor Palmer and his secretary.

Steven and Carissa were already friends. These close, isolated quarters they were stuck in turned a good friendship into something more. Normally this could be a very pleasing beautiful thing yet, their relationship was about to become something ugly. A relationship that was less than God's very best for either of them.

One night, Steve decided to work late. He had sent Carissa home. Nevertheless, a drenched Carissa came back clopping into the church building sobbing, "My boyfriend Nicholas dumped me tonight on the very night I expected he was going to propose to me. If that wasn't bad enough my landlord says, "I'm late on my rent and if I don't pay up, I'm out on the street." said Carissa. Steve held her in a comforting manner.

Carissa asked Steve, "Why can't more men be like you? You are so nice." Then she kissed him. Without thinking he embraced her affectionately; he could see miles away where this was going to lead. He loves the Lord and didn't want to dishonor God. Yet, he loved Carissa, as a friend. Carissa was someone Steve could see himself ending up with. Nevertheless, he knew taking advantage of her would just be wrong. Knowing this he still crossed the line he knew he should never cross. That next morning, they woke with regret.

They were bare naked in each other's arms. They cared for each other yet, they knew they had made a horrible mistake. Steve had taken advantage of a woman who he deeply cared for and Carissa realized she has just destroyed the career of her pastor, not to mention how it hurt Steve's spiritual health.

"Oh, Carissa I'm so sorry for taking advantage of you when you were in such a vulnerable state.", apologized Steve. Then Carissa assured him that she forgave him and that she recognized that she too wasn't thinking she said, "I shouldn't have come to see you. I have girlfriends I could have talked to them; about all the trouble I'm having. But I meant what I said, I do care for you and I want to meet a guy like you. However, I didn't want to ruin our professional relationship by pursuing a romantic relationship with you and now I've done the very thing I have been trying to avoid worse, I have thrown away our purity.

They tried to forget that it ever happened. However, forgetting wasn't easy. Neither of them believed sex should be treated as casual. Thus, they each turn to trusted friends. Carissa asked her friend Megan out for coffee and Steve confessed his sin to his mentor. Carissa met her friend at a little café in downtown Hartlin. She sat at an outdoor table. Carissa's heart beat nervously louder and louder as her friend approached in her white flowered sundress. Fearing that her friend would reject her.

Carissa already felt like dirt and was beating herself up. Megan said, "What's up girl? You sound worried?" With tears Carissa sobbed, "Meg, I made a horrible mistake. I slept with my boss." "Who, you don't mean that Pastor do you?" Asked Megan. Carissa replied, "yes and I feel so dirty."

Megan angrily asked, "Did that jerk force himself on you?" Carissa then said, "No, no you don't understand Steve was a total gentleman and it was completely consensual." Her friend was not a believer and therefore didn't hold purity in such high regard, in fact she felt it was about time Carissa give into her carnal desires. Carissa took Megan's words with a grain of salt but, she knew as a daughter of her father God. God wants more from her then to treat her virginity so flippantly.

Steve, he didn't want to but, he knew he needed to get advice from his mentor so he made an appointment with Rev. Warren and met with him at his office. Rev. Warren's secretary said, "Pastor sensed you were going to call and that I should free up this afternoon for you two, to talk and pray."

When Steve arrived at Scott's office, Rev. Warren told Steve to sit down and he asked, "Pastor what is up?" Steve responded in tears, "last night I had sex with my secretary. I didn't mean for it to happen, it just happened."

Scott just sat there silently listening and thinking of what he ought to say. To Steve the silence felt like it was going to go on forever. He feared that his act of sexual immorality had gone too far. Was Rev. Warren going to reject him, and treat him like a worldly and perverse heathen? He knew he would deserve shunning but, he so hoped for mercy. When Rev. Warren finally spoke, he said, "oh dear son of mine I'm so sorry. I forgive you and I can assure you Jesus; your Lord and groom has forgiven you.

It is true you have sinned and there are consequences to your actions. You have upset the Lord and dishonored your own body and the body of your sister in the Lord. By not running when the enemy tempted you with sex. You have let Satan in and he will attack your ministry. Yet you already know this."

Knowing that Steve had to be beating himself up Scott knew that condonation wasn't what he needed. So, he said, "Listen, Steve yes you made a horrible mistake but, like the Samaritan woman at the well, who was living in sin with a man she wasn't married to. However, God, used her to bring many Samaritans to Jesus. In the same way God, can and still will use you. Nevertheless, you must confess your sin to your congregation and ask for their forgiveness.

It was a rough week for Carissa and Steve. They were embarrassed at what they had allowed to happen. If this had been the worst consequence that had come out of their affair, they could have gotten over it. Unfortunately, things only went downhill. Within days each of them started to get very malicious calls.

It all started one afternoon at the office, when a woman called Carissa. She answered the phone and her normal sweet and friendly voice, "good afternoon, St. Thomas Church." Carissa said, "How may I help you?" Then the woman screamed, "You little whore how dare you seduce our pastor! I wish we were back in the Old Testament times so I could stone sluts like you!" Carissa dropped the phone and started sobbing. Pastor Palmer heard her crying and he asked, "What is going on, why are you crying?" Carissa told him about the woman who had called.

What they didn't realize is that Carissa's friend Megan hadn't been much of a friend. She had spread the gossip all around Hartlin. When a fire of gossip gets going it doesn't take long particularly in a small town like Hartlin before everyone thinks they know what's going on. As a result, of the explosive gossip, the calls kept coming in and Steve had no choice but to call an emergency board meeting to deal with the rumors.

Steve opened the meeting by saying, "I have called you here because I have a confession to make. Some of you may have heard the rumors that I have had sex with Carissa. I'm sorry to say, but this is true. Yes, I care for her greatly and never intended for this to happen."

I have apologized to her and now I would like to ask for your forgiveness. However, I do understand that this does not excuse my actions and I will accept any punishment I must face. Bud the youngest board member was the roughest on Steve. He said, "Listen my brothers and sisters I know what it is like to be caught up in the beauty of a bodacious babe but, as my pastor I expected more of you. If you can't control yourself, you shouldn't be our pastor." Nick on the other hand was more forgiving. He was a biblical scholar however, he himself had made mistakes for which he had paid dearly. So, he said, "brother bud is correct. Our spiritual leader must not be so weak that he is taken out by the first pretty face that gives him the time of day. Yet, I plead with you brothers and sisters to show compassion to our pastor clearly, he is repentant.

The board prayed about what should be done about the situation. Then they voted and the board came out 4 to 6 in favor of Pastor Palmer staying. The board decided Steve could stay on probationally if he agrees to apologize to the congregation publicly and of course avoid being alone with women. Steve agreed to these terms, since he didn't like the idea of being alone with Carissa in the first place. Nevertheless, he felt his church was going to easy on him. So, he asked if he could please take a self-imposed unpaid suspension.

That Sunday when Pastor Palmer got up to speak instead of giving a normal sermon he said, "in the Word, it says we must confess your sins to one another. But, how many of us do this? I as your pastor realize I need to set the example. So here it goes. As some of you may have heard, and I'm sure many of you have. Judging by how many people are missing today. I found myself in a rather compromising situation, and I gave into temptation. I have not honored God, this church, my own body and I have dishonored the woman who I had sex with."

With this a commotion broke out. Everyone was in shock when they heard these words. Some people had heard the rumors but I had dismissed them as nasty slander. Still others had heard nothing. Thus, nobody knew what to make of Pastor Palmer's word.

Pastor Palmer then said, "What I have done is inexcusable but, I ask you for your forgiveness. Please do not hold my sins against the local church body. It is true that I am the leader of this body and the Lord will judge me harsher than you because I hold a leadership position yet, I am just a human as you are.

I will be taking some time off to pray, and seek God's direction about the situation." Pastor Steve Palmer's sin hurt St. Thomas Church. They lost half of its members just because of this incident alone.

Discussion Questions

1. Why do we keep on doing the things we know we shouldn't do and avoid the things we should do? Why do we have to be so careful to avoid the appearance of wrong doing?

2. What should the board have done when Steve pleaded not to be left alone with Carissa? How might you be able to relate the situation to your own life?

3. When Carissa came in wet and distraught what should Steve have done?

4. How should you treat those in your congregation who sin? (John 8:1-11, Matthew 18:15-35, 7:1-5)

5. Why does it matter where we get our advice from? (Proverbs 2:12-15, 1 Timothy 1:3-7)

Epilogue

Edna lived just long enough to see pastor palmer return to the pulpit. Her friends and family remembered her as a shining example of what a child of God should look like. She was met by God the father who, when he saw her, he kissed her on the cheek as only a father can.

The Mitchell's grew in love for one another and in the Lord. It took Jason until his second year in college before he accepted the Lord. Amber and Gregory stayed close and soon after college they married and became missionaries to Amsterdam. Jason went on to plant the second church that came out of St. Thomas Church.

As a result, of their affair, Carrissa became pregnant, Steve offered to marry her but, she wasn't able to forgive herself for the affair and she turned Steve down. She moved away for she was unable to face her friends in Hartlin anymore.

Steve continued to serve his flock after a month of fasting and prayer. He held the position of senior pastor of St. Thomas church once again until his death at the ripe old age of 108 years. Reader(s) of this book, I have talked a lot about what the church ought to look like but it can all be summarized with this one verse. "Now these three remain hope, faith and love. But, the greatest of these is love." (1 Corinthians 13:13) *

It is easy to criticize people for doing wrong. What is hard is to forgive and to love other people we encounter. Yet, if we the church, don't, the church has no hope to survive. However, God's 135 word is clear, the church will last forever which, I can only assume, means that the church can and will love the world as Jesus has. Nevertheless, it still is up to each one of us to love the people we meet every day as Jesus would.

Resources and Work cited

http://autismmythbusters.com/general-public/famous-autistic-people/   http://www.biblestudytools.com/   http://www.dailymail.co.uk/health/article-2521032/Dan-Aykroyd-I-Aspergers—symptoms-included-obsessed-ghosts.html   htttp://www.mops.org Nathan,

Rich. Who is My Enemy?. Grand Rapids: Zondervan, 2002.

Neurodivergent and Neurotypical, www.dictionary.com